About the Book

MONSTERS . . . even the word
sounds *scary*. They come in many
shapes and sizes. Usually they are big
and bad, but some monsters are small
and gentle.

Long ago, people all over the world
believed in dragons and ogres, giants
and demons, and they told strange
stories about monsters they had outwitted or destroyed.

In *13 Monsters* you will read some
of these exciting old tales—of a
dreadful, scaly creature called the
Deerhurst Worm, or a huge and gentle cow that never went dry, or the
fierce Ogress Grana whose hot breath
could wither a corn field.

These tales are some of the fasci-
nating stories which were told to
Dorothy Gladys Spicer by people
who now live in regions where the
legends were actually born. They are
marvelous stories and no matter how
much monsters make you shiver, they
are fun to read about.

13 MONSTERS

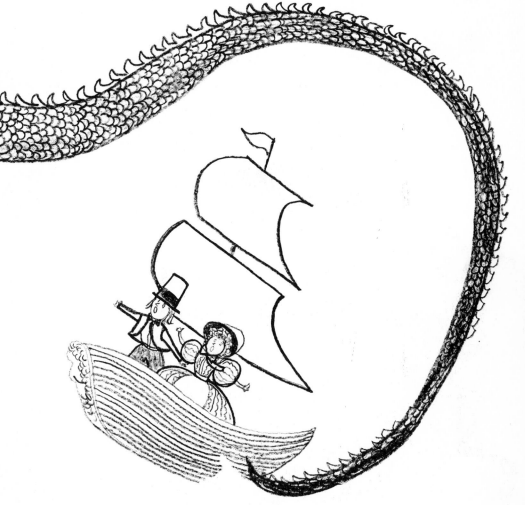

by

DOROTHY GLADYS SPICER

illustrated by Sofia

COWARD-McCANN, Inc.   NEW YORK

Also by Dorothy Gladys Spicer

46 DAYS OF CHRISTMAS

13 WITCHES

5755

CONTENTS

To
HERMAN-EGBERT STEL and
SUZANNA GERARDA STEL-WESTERMANN

and

the kind people of *mooi Drenthe*

ABOUT MONSTERS

MONSTERS . . . even the word prickles the spine. "Monster" comes from the Latin verb *monere,* meaning "to warn." So I'm warning you, Beware of monsters!

Monsters are cunning creatures. They come in many shapes and sizes. Usually we picture monsters as big and bad—but there are small ones, too. There are also monsters who are gentle and good. In *13 Monsters,* you'll find several varieties of monsters—big and little, good and bad.

Long, long ago, men all over the world believed in dragons and giants, ogres, demons and beasts of prodigious size. Once people thought that such creatures bewitched them, that they stole sheep, and ravaged the land. That's why folk began telling stories about monsters they'd outwitted, or slain by stealth. I've often heard tales like these— in lands where people remember their monster myths. And I've learned that they once thought of robber barons as fierce dragons, and disasters of sea and storm as giants' handiwork.

In *13 Monsters,* I've told a few of these exciting old yarns. Some stories I've gathered in places that monsters still are supposed to haunt! Other tales I have heard—or read—here and there. All of the stories are mine in the telling—though they have come down through hundreds of years.

I hope you'll like my monsters. No matter how much they make you shiver, monsters are fun to read about.

—DOROTHY GLADYS SPICER

7

1

THE BOGLE GHOST OF BARRA BOG
(Scotland)

Long, long ago, in the Highlands of Scotland, there was once a young fiddler named Danny MacPherson. No one thought of celebrating a wedding, or a harvest homing, without Danny to make the music. He was the finest musician for miles about. When he tucked his fiddle under his chin and his bow sang upon the strings, old and young tapped their toes. Soon everything that breathed was dancing—even the mice in the walls.

At every feast or party it was, "One more dance, Danny. Danny, play one more." That's why it always was late when the youth passed Barra Bog, going home from doings the far side of the glen.

It never occurred to Danny that he was in danger, not until Deacon Fergus warned him—the night of Rosie Magillivray's ball. Of course, Danny had heard rumors of a ghost who haunted the place betwixt sundown and cockcrow. But the youth was too easygoing to set stock in such tales. *He'd* never seen any ghost or spirit, though he'd passed the bog a hundred times.

All Danny cared about was his fiddle—and earning enough for that small farm in the valley. Once he'd done *that*, he planned to ask Jeanie to be his wife.

Danny's eyes followed her slim figure now, as she danced with Hugh Donaldson. She looked so bonnie in her new red frock—black curls flying, cheeks like a rose. The lads hovered over her like bees over heather on the moors. She danced first with this youth, then with that. But Danny wished she'd dance less with Hugh Donaldson. Hugh had just inherited his father's farm. He was a man of substance now, and looking about for a wife. It made Danny uneasy, the way Hugh's eyes never left Jeanie's face, whether dancing with her or not.

When Danny stopped playing, Jeanie joined him. It was then that Deacon Fergus walked toward them, a worried look on his kind

9

face. "Look here, you two," he said. "I've got to talk with Danny. And as for you, lass"—he pinched Jeanie's cheek affectionately—"dare an old man hope for the next dance?"

"All he has to do is *ask!*" cried Jeanie as she walked away laughing.

The deacon came close to Danny. "You'd best not go home through the glen tonight," he told him in a low voice. "Don't risk passing Barra Bog. Folks about here say the bogle ghost who haunts it is up to nasty tricks."

"The bogle ghost!" cried Danny, his blue eyes sparkling. "Now tell me, Deacon, whatever's a *bogle?* And why should one scare me into walking home two extra miles, by a dark rough road?"

Though he pretended to know nothing of bogles, the youth remembered hearing of them as a child. His grandmother had warned him against the mischievous sprites. They whined in the walls after dark, she said. They tapped on windowpanes. And worst of all, they tweaked little boys' noses when they told fibs!

"Now listen to me, lad," said the deacon sternly, for he loved Danny like a son. "This isn't for joking. Bogles are real—and so are their ghosts. *Living* bogles aren't bad—though a nuisance. They let the mares out at night, hide the egg money, and steal gooseberry tarts from the larder shelf. But *dead* bogles are different," he went on, his hand on Danny's arm. "There's no telling what *they* will do. They grow taller and meaner the older they get. People say the bogle ghost of the bog is big as a barn!"

Danny laughed as he picked up his fiddle. "I'll remember what you've said," he promised, giving the old man's shoulder an affectionate pat. "But if I don't get back to the fiddling now, I won't earn a farthing to carry home."

As Danny drew his bow across the strings, youths pulled rosy-cheeked lassies to their toes. Soon the old rafters shook with the stampings and whirlings of eager feet. The lad, moved by the magic of his lusty tunes, swayed his tall body in time to the music.

"Danny's a fine young man," the deacon told Jeanie when he claimed his dance, "though he never was one to heed advice from his elders! Aside from you and his fiddle, a serious thought never roosted under that thatch of red hair." The deacon sighed as he told the girl about the ghost, and the danger of the bog.

10

That night Danny was later than usual when he started home. He was whistling as he entered the glen. He'd already forgotten the deacon and his warnings of bogle ghosts. Danny's heart was bursting with joy. Jeanie had been so sweet when she'd said good night. She had let him kiss her, right before Hugh—which should settle *his* notions about her.

Danny jingled the silver that weighed down his pocket. "If things keep on like tonight," he told an owl in a tree, "I can ask Jeanie to marry me soon."

Thoughts of Jeanie as his wife in a little home of their own so warmed the lad's heart that he whistled louder than ever. He didn't notice he was passing the bog until he heard slogging footsteps. Then he glanced up sharply. What Danny saw froze his blood. For there, advancing toward him across the spongy earth, was a huge white-clad figure, with a club in each hand. Danny couldn't see the face beneath the white hood—only eyes that gleamed like lanterns in the dark.

It's the bogle ghost, the youth thought wildly, remembering the deacon's warning too late. He's headed for me . . . with two clubs. Each one's big enough to kill an ox! Terrified though he was, Danny wasn't one to run away. He slipped his fiddle behind a rock. Then he clenched his fists in case he had to use them. He stepped forward shouting, "Who are you?"

"The Bogle Ghost of Barra Bog," bellowed the creature, striding toward Danny with long steps. "Even such a fool as you should know *that*! Up to now, I've been patient. I've never knocked you down —though your feet shake my bog, your whistles disturb my sleep. But this time, you'll have to fight to get by my place. I'll teach you who's master here."

"I'm not scared to fight a skinny old ghost like you," Danny yelled, though by now he quaked in his boots.

"Brave words," sneered the ghost with a chilling laugh. "You'll live to regret them, you cocksure young fiddler. Here, take this club," the ghost roared. He marched up to Danny, clapping one of the cudgels in his hand. "I want a fair fight—wouldn't want it said it wasn't. Defend yourself—if you can!"

The bogle backed off. When he started twirling his club over his head, Danny knew he was going to attack. The next second the ghost flew at him. He dealt out blows that almost sent the lad sprawl-

11

ing. But Danny thwacked back steadily until the bogle howled with pain. When he lifted his club to crack the youth's skull, Danny rushed at him with such fury that the bogle dropped his club. Then Danny slugged at the monster again and again, thinking to snap the thin body in two. Instead, it whirled round and round like a top.

When the bogle had spun to the brink of the bog, he toppled into it with a horrible shriek. Still shrieking, he sank into the wet swampy ground until Danny could see nothing but the white-hooded head, and the ghastly light from the burning eyes.

"You've beaten me this time," shrilled the ghost. "But wait, young man, just you wait! Bogles never give up. I'll have revenge yet."

"That you won't," bawled Danny, brandishing his cudgel. "If you dare try it, *I'll knock you dead.*"

After the bogle had vanished, Danny snatched up his fiddle. Then he ran from the glen as fast as he could. By the time he'd reached home, it was almost time to get up. The cock had crowed. Light streaked the sky. Danny's face was scratched and bruised. Every bone in his body jumped with pain. As the youth staggered into bed and pulled the covers over his head, he muttered, "I won't tell a soul what happened tonight—not even my mother. The deacon would hear of it. After his warning, folks would think me a fool."

Danny fell asleep at once. But even in his sleep he could see the monster's baleful eyes. In the morning when his mother asked about his bruises, Danny said he'd stumbled and fallen in the dark, coming home.

Jeanie rushed into his arms when *she* saw his face. "Danny, Danny," she sobbed. "You *did* pass the bog, after all Deacon Fergus said! It's a wonder the bogle didn't kill you!"

Danny held the girl closely. He planted a kiss on her shining curls. At first he wouldn't admit that he'd met the ghost. But when Jeanie pressed him, Danny confessed his adventure in the glen. Then he made her promise not to tell anyone.

"Deacon Fergus thinks me featherbrained as it is," he told her. "I did forget his warning—though I won't again!"

In the days and weeks that followed, everyone knew Jeanie favored Danny, though she flirted with Hugh. Danny's fiddling was so popular for balls and parties that the old woolen sock under his mattress soon bulged with coins. Still he was stubborn. He wouldn't propose to

Jeanie, Danny told his mother, until he'd saved enough for the farm.

"I'll soon have it," the lad said with a warm smile. "Then I'll ask Jeanie to be my wife."

"Why not ask her now?" suggested his mother, glancing up from her mending. "The lass loves *you*, son, not that farm. She'll wait for you, once you've told her you want her. But if you don't, remember, plenty of boys have an eye on Jeanie—and her father has plans!"

In spite of everything his mother said, Danny decided he wouldn't ask Jeanie—*yet*. It wasn't until weeks later, after he'd scrimped and scraped until he had leather patches on his elbows, and holes in his shoes, that his mother heard a wild whoop. She ran to the door, to see Danny rushing down the lane with his fiddle.

"I've enough, Mother, enough at last!" the youth cried, tossing his cap into the air. "I've counted my savings the five hundredth time. *I'm asking Jeanie tonight*—after the ball. Wish me luck!"

"Good luck, son," his mother called, waving as her handsome son bounded out of sight. "And I hope you aren't too late," she murmured, returning to the stove.

That night Danny was in such gay spirits that the dancers cheered him wildly. Jeanie came in late, with Hugh as her escort. She gave Hugh every dance, Danny noted uneasily. He'd never seen her cheeks so pink, her hair so pretty. He longed to take the girl in his arms. Yet Danny could see something was wrong. Every time he tried to catch Jeanie's attention, she glanced away quickly. Once there were tears in her eyes.

When it came time to stop fiddling, Danny decided he wouldn't wait until later to propose to Jeanie. He'd ask her now! But just as he started to find her, Deacon Fergus held him back.

"Wait, lad," he said. "I have something to tell you before you go to Jeanie. The girl loves you—she as much as told me so. But her father, who wants her married, said you'd never get around to asking her."

"But I—I'm going to—*now*," stammered Danny, sensing disaster.

"Yes, yes, Danny," the deacon said. "But don't you understand, boy, *you're too late*! You've kept putting off proposing. The girl gave in to her father. She's already said yes to Hugh!"

"To Hugh!" Danny repeated dully. "*Hugh*! No—it can't be.

14

She doesn't love *him*. She loves me. I couldn't ask a girl to marry me until I had a home. And now—"

"And now," said the deacon gently, "if you love Jeanie you'll not try to see her tonight. You'd make a scene. She'd burst into tears. But don't give up hope, lad," the old man said, stepping closer. "Why don't you go to Jeanie's father tomorrow? Tell him you've *worked* for your farm. After all, Hugh *inherited* his! Tell Jeanie's father you love her, how much she loves you. There's still a chance—if he wants to see his daughter happy."

Danny was so miserable he never knew how he managed to play the rest of the evening. When the ball was over, he slipped away without speaking to Jeanie. He stumbled home on feet of lead. Danny ached so for Jeanie that he knew he couldn't live without her. Why did he always have to be pigheaded? Why hadn't he listened to his mother's advice?

The youth was so wrapped in bitter thoughts that at first he didn't notice where he was. When he saw he was passing the bog he didn't even care. Nothing mattered now he'd lost Jeanie—not even a ghost.

At that very moment the wicked bogle, still smarting from defeat, heard Danny's footsteps. The wraith, who was slipping in and out among the rocks opposite the bog, paused to listen. "Ah—ha!" he cried, gleefully rubbing his bony hands. "So the young fool is back again. I've waited weeks to catch him. This time I won't give him a chance to fight back. I'll grab him by a leg and toss his worthless carcass into the river."

The bogle peered toward Danny. Then, coiling his long body like a snake, he waited for his victim from behind a rock. Danny, unaware of his danger, plodded along with dejected steps. He was thinking of Jeanie as he crashed to the ground. His fiddle flew out of his hands but fell into a pile of leaves.

"Now I've got you," screeched the ghost, gripping the lad's leg, "and *I'm going to kill you!*"

The ghost's cold breath chilled Danny's whole body. The dreadful eyes flamed with hate. Before Danny could strike out with his fists, the bogle had grabbed him like a sack of meal. With a howl of triumph the creature slung Danny to his shoulder. Then the bogle strode to the ravine.

With the strength of ten men the monster pitched his victim toward the river. "I'll drown you, I'll drown you," he yelled. Then he laughed so wildly that Danny couldn't hear the waters roar.

It wasn't long before the ghost's laughter turned to mutters of fury. For as Danny hurtled downward, his belt caught in the limbs of a tree growing straight from the rocks. A branch hooked through his belt, holding him fast. There he dangled above the river. This is luck, Danny thought, as the ghost prepared to attack him. My hands are free. At least I can fight back.

The bogle zoomed toward Danny with a wicked hiss. Then the ghost kicked with both feet. "So a brittle branch keeps you from drowning," he yelled in fury. "I'll take care of that! In another second you'll be mincemeat. I'll feed you to the fishes, one bite at a time."

Though the ghost pommeled Danny harder than ever, the youth managed, somehow, to yank the hunting knife from his belt. As the bogle backed away to inflict a fierce blow on his head, Danny shot out his arm. He pierced the ghost once, then twice. Each time, the point of the knife ripped through the thin body as if it were paper. No blood gushed from the wounds, though the ghost screamed with pain. When Danny struck him the third time, the bogle fell backward with a wail that echoed up and down the ravine like the howling of wind. Then he plopped into the water.

Even then, Danny wasn't certain the bogle was dead—at least, not until he peered down at the river. Then he saw the waters reach toward the body. They clutched the ghost's robe with greedy fingers, then sucked him down, down into the swirling foam.

After he'd seen the monster die, Danny felt too weak to move. He closed his eyes. When Deacon Fergus and his men searched the glen next day, they found the fiddle among the leaves. "The lad must be here *somewhere*," said the old man as he picked it up. It wasn't long before they found Danny, only half-conscious, still hanging by his belt from the limb of the tree.

"My fiddle—the bogle ghost," Danny murmured as his rescuers laid him on the ground. "He's dead . . . drowned. I stabbed him—then —then—"

"The boy burns with fever," one man said, shaking his head.
"Nobody *ever* kills a ghost," declared a second.
"Especially a *bogle*," a third added.

16

"He's out of his head," the first man said, wiping the sweat from Danny's brow.

"*Is* he, though?" shouted the deacon. He held up a white shred the youth clutched in his fingers. "Tell me, what do you call *this?*"

The men crowded round the deacon. They stared in silence at the shred. Then they drew back in horror.

"That's—that's—*shroud stuff*," ventured one man, blanching.

"It's not man-made," another whispered.

"Only a ghost—ever—wears the likes of this!" a third cried, his voice shaking.

"Aye," said the deacon, gazing from one to another. "You're *all* right. This scrap doesn't really *prove* Danny's killed the bogle ghost. But it *is* ghost shroud cloth—and if the bogle is never seen again, *that's* proof."

The men carried Danny home to his mother. They laid him on his bed, and his fiddle where he could see it when he opened his eyes. For days he tossed with fever. He moaned strange things about the ghost. He kept calling for Jeanie. After the days had stretched into weeks, his mother's broths and Jeanie's tender words restored Danny to health.

When Jeanie confessed that *she* had sent the deacon to search for him in the glen, Danny realized how much the girl loved him. "When your mother told me you hadn't come home after the ball, I knew you were in trouble. I told the deacon how you'd thrashed the bogle, the night you forgot and went by the bog. I know I promised not to tell," she sobbed, as Danny put his arms around her, "but this time, I was s-sure you were dead."

"And so I should be," cried Danny, hugging Jeanie, "if you'd kept your promise. But now I'm going to see your father," he said, starting for the lane.

"I want to marry Jeanie," Danny told her father, without wasting time. "I love her, and she loves me. I can take care of her, too," the youth added with pride. "I wouldn't ask her to be my wife until I could."

The older man studied Danny's face with twinkling eyes. Then he threw back his head and laughed. "A lad who can kill a bogle ghost —alone at night in the glen—can take care of my Jeanie," he cried, thumping Danny on the back. "I'm proud of you, son. But what about Hugh?"

"Jeanie never loved *him*," said Danny. "You've known that all along. And I know Hugh wouldn't want to marry a girl who doesn't love him. With that farm from his father, he can have his pick of a dozen pretty girls—so long as he leaves my Jeanie alone!"

When Danny MacPherson had wed his own bonnie lass, every man, woman and bairn for miles around rejoiced. The youth took Jeanie to the small farm in the valley. There they lived forever after, the happiest couple in the land.

And as for the bogle ghost—no one ever saw the horrid creature again. The pride of Highland folk in Danny was wide as the moors. "The finest fiddler in these parts," they boasted. "Our finest hero, as well."

2

ELLERT'S FIELD AND BRAMMERT'S HEAP

(Netherlands)

I

Once upon a time, in northeastern Holland, wicked giants flourished in *mooi Drenthe,* beautiful Drenthe—the inland province that ends to the east at the German frontier. Long ago, Drenthe was a vast swamp. Today the land is rich in wheat and rye. The wide moors unfurl in the splendor of purple heather, the glow of golden gorse.

In Drenthe you see many strange things. But strangest of all are the *hunnebedden,* the beds where giants sleep under piles of vast boulders.

For thousands of years the giants' mysterious graves have dotted Drenthe's heaths. The stones tower one on another, and yet another, so you might think they'd topple to earth. Yet nothing topples the stones. Giant hands placed them on the heath, long ago. There they will stay till the end of time. Only the *Witte Wieven,* the White Women of Mist who dance around the graves on nights in spring, know where the giants got their stones, and how they balanced them over their dead.

Back in the days of Drenthe's giants, none were so evil as Ellert and Brammert, a father and son. They robbed and murdered the helpless and weak. Dutch children still speak the giants' names in terror. They lived in a dank turf hut they had dug with their huge hands from the heath that people call *Ellertsveld,* or Ellert's Field, to this day.

Pines and birches now border the heath, where bees gather honey and skylarks sing with exceeding sweetness. But long, long ago, the place was desolate and still. The field was a vast plain. It rolled from the door of the hovel toward the village of Orvelterveen. In those days the heather blossomed blood-red. No trees surrounded the heath. No bees, no birds, lived there. Only the hungry vultures circled overhead.

19

Dreadful things happened on the lonely heath when Ellert and Brammert were alive. The giants lured the unwary to certain death. Their victims' bleached bones lay scattered on the field, their possessions on the dirt floor of the hut.

To snare their prey, the giants devised a deathtrap so cunning no man escaped. Around the fringe of the heath, they strung small iron bells on threads, so fine and dark you hardly saw them. Then Ellert and Brammert wove them in and out of the heather branches. If passers-by even *touched* the heather, the bells set up a wild clangor of noise.

Once they'd woven their awful web, Ellert and Brammert crouched inside their hut. There they listened, their matted heads bent until their beards swept the floor. At the bells' first signal, the giants leaped to their feet.

"Quick, Brammert," the old giant bellowed, grabbing the cudgel at his feet. "Out to the heath. We've trapped a stranger."

"And he'd better be rich!" Brammert rumbled, rubbing spit on his palms. "That stupid fellow we snared last night didn't have a copper in his pantaloons."

"Come along," Ellert growled, bending double to get out of the door. "We've no time to waste. Follow me to the edge of the heath."

As Brammert strode behind his father, his black eyes glittered with greed. He toyed with the club made from an oak he had pulled like a twig from the ground. "A rich burgomaster with a gold watch and chain—that's the booty I'd like."

It never took the giants long to cover the heath, for Ellert and Brammert were three times as tall as ordinary men. When the father and son found a victim snared in the strong tentacles of thread, they howled with laughter. They threatened him with taunts and yells when he struggled to lift his feet.

"Welcome to Ellert's Field," the old giant always roared before hitting the hapless one on the head. Brammert finished off their victim when he cried for mercy.

One evening when the giants had trapped a stranger, they stripped his pockets of trinkets, ripped the silver buttons from his jacket, and took his fur cap—even the red cotton kerchief from his pocket. Then Brammert tossed the body to the vultures which screamed for their feast.

20

Back in the dark cave, Ellert and Brammert stooped over their plunder. They poked dirty black fingernails through the loot they'd snatched.

"Ho, I only got a knife with a broken blade," Brammert shouted in rage.

"I've found a silver florin in this old leather purse," his father gloated, biting the coin in his teeth. "And look here—if these aren't coppers, so old they're green!"

The giant rattled the coins to the floor. He counted them eagerly. "One—two—three—four—five—six—*seven*," he shouted in triumph.

"Well, a florin and seven coppers are something," Brammert grunted enviously. "What *I* want is a watch!"

One day, when Ellert and Brammert were listening for the usual frenzied crashing of the bells, they heard an extraordinary sound. "Did you hear that?" Ellert shouted, pushing the hair from his eyes.

His son—who'd sprawled full length on the floor since he'd devoured a goose, beak, bones, feathers and all—quickly propped himself on his elbow. "Ha, I hear music!" Brammert cried. "Our bells are playing a tune!" He beat the air with his filthy forefinger, in time to a musical tingtanging from over the heath.

The sound was sweet as if an elfin hand were playing chimes in a village church. The listening giants stared at each other. "Someone's out there," Ellert said slowly. "Yet who can it be? What we hear isn't the mad furor of the bells when a stranger's ensnared in the web."

"There's booty out there, the likes of which we've never found," Brammert cried, his bloodshot eyes glowing fiercely. "Come, Father, come," he urged, springing to his feet.

The giants tightened their belts. They pulled on their high boots. As they hurried from the hut, Ellert pointed toward Orvelterveen. "The sound is from that way," he shouted, starting across the heath at a lope.

II

Now as the two giants sped toward the tingtanging, Marchien, a young peasant girl from the village, sat in the heather at the edge of the heath. She was laughing gaily, unaware that danger was closing about her. In either hand the girl held a thread strung with bells.

If only her mother could hear this pretty music, thought Marchien, she'd not forbid her to come here. Why had she—and her grandmother, too—always warned against the bells on the heath? Ever since she was little, Marchien had wanted to find out about them for herself. Such silly talk about a trap set with bells by fierce giants who murdered for money! Yet for all the babble, no one from Orvelterveen had ever been snared, had even *heard* the bells, or *seen* the giants! People always gossiped about unknown strangers who were victims. Folk from *her* village never went near the heath. They were too frightened to find out things for themselves, thought Marchien, pulling two threads at once.

The young girl soon discovered she could play tunes with the bells. She tried the one Rieks, the lad from the next farm, always hummed when he took her home from the fields. At thought of his kind, sun-tanned face, his hair bleached to the color of tow, Marchien smiled tenderly. "I think Rieks will ask me to marry him, come Easter," she murmured.

The girl's cheeks glowed pinker, her eyes brighter, as she coaxed the bells into a rustic dance. She was in Rieks' arms now. Her entire body swayed in rhythm with the tune.

By now Marchien was so absorbed in the music that she didn't hear the thumpity-thump-thump of the giants' feet pounding across the field. It wasn't until the earth where she was sitting began to heave that the girl glanced up. When she saw the two wild-eyed creatures racing toward her, huge clubs in their hands, Marchien shrieked in horror. She released the threads so suddenly that the bells jangled in wild discordant notes. Poor Marchien was so terrified she was rooted to the heath. She threw her apron over her head and crouched down in the heather, sobbing wildly.

"Ah—*ha*, what have we here?" Ellert roared, poking at the shaking girl with his toe.

"A beautiful booty, Father," yelled Brammert with a snort of pleasure. "We've found something finer than gold!"

"Get up, daughter of man," Ellert ordered, shaking Marchien's shoulder. "Tell us who you are—where you come from. How dare you meddle with our bells?"

Marchien, still too paralyzed to even glance at the giants, sobbed harder than ever. When Brammert growled, "If you don't stop

whimpering, I'll bash in your silly head," she dropped the apron from her face.

"I-I meant no harm. I-I'm only Marchien," she faltered, brushing her tears with the back of her hand. "I'm a poor peasant girl from Or-Orvelterveen. I haven't a p-penny to give you," she added, remembering she'd heard the giants wanted money. "I only want to go h-home to my mother!"

"Your mother, eh? Father, did you hear that?" shouted Brammert, slapping his thigh so hard that Marchien jumped. "You'd better forget your mother, girl. You'll never see *her* again. You'll go home with us—unless we decide to kill you on the spot."

"You don't think we'd let a pretty prize like you slip through our fingers?" Ellert bawled, yanking Marchien to her feet.

Marchien clasped her hands tightly, hoping the giants wouldn't notice how they shook. "So, it *is* true," the girl said, staring at one giant, then the other. "Everything Mother told me is true. It wasn't just a made-up story to keep me from having fun, when she warned me of giants, and forbade my going to the heath."

Marchien began crying again when she thought of how she had disobeyed her mother. She had peered at the heath from far away, then crept along the edges. She told lies when her mother asked where she'd been. And now—

"Stop that sniveling, girl of Orvelterveen," bellowed Ellert, snatching up her wrist so it ached. When Marchien tried to yank away, the old giant picked her up like a kitten and tucked her, kicking and screaming, under one arm. "I told you to *stop*!" Ellert growled, giving Marchien a shake. "Listen to me, girl. We won't kill you. We won't even hurt you—if you behave."

"And if you don't, remember my club!" Brammert threatened, dashing his cudgel at a boulder so the stone shattered to a thousand bits.

"It's no use making a fuss," Ellert cried, striding toward the hut. "Nobody can hear you. You're going home with us—to cook our food, mend our clothes, take care of our house."

"I—cook, mend, clean—for two dirty giants! *Never*," Marchien shrieked, trying to bite the giant's hand.

"Mind your tongue—*and* your manners," Ellert yelled, with another shake. "You'll go as our housekeeper, with no more screams and howls, or the vultures will get a meal."

24

Brammert howled with laughter to see his father scowl at the girl so his brows bristled like the quills on a porcupine. "Which will it be?" Ellert demanded, so fiercely Marchien cringed.

Marchien knew she had no choice but to go with the giants if she wanted to live. There would always be a chance of escape. They'd miss her in the village. Someone would come. *Why* hadn't she heeded her mother! Why did she have to learn too late? But there wasn't time for regrets now. The giants were eying her. They were waiting for her answer.

"I-I'll go with you peaceably," Marchien stammered, trying to keep the quaver from her voice. "I won't cry again. I won't make a fuss."

"Now you're talking sense," Ellert rumbled, setting Marchien on her feet. "You do know what's good for you, after all. Our hut's yonder, the other side of the heath."

When they reached the door of the giants' hovel, Marchien stifled a scream. She stared at the entrance, low even for her, at the turfs piled one on another for walls, at the roof of fir branches with heather growing on top.

"What's the matter?" snarled Ellert, watching the girl from narrowed eyes. "Isn't our house grand enough for you?"

"Oh, yes," Marchien hastily replied. "It's—it's just that *it's part of the heath.*"

"That it is," laughed Brammert, relishing the joke. "No one can tell what's hut, what's heath—in case you have notions of people finding you here!"

Inside their hovel the giants displayed huge caldrons and pots. The hearth was stuffed with ashes. Bones and feathers littered the dirt floor. "You'll have to earn your keep," thundered Ellert, thrusting a faggot broom at the shaking girl. "Get to work. Clean up the place."

Marchien didn't know where to start. She peered into dark corners, thinking of rats. She gazed at the holes that served as windows. The giants were watching her closely. "We can see out north, south, east and west," Ellert said with a grin. "It's well to remember—if anyone foolishly tries to escape."

Despair swept over Marchien. She could see the spire of the village church—so near, yet so far. At sundown, she thought she could hear chimes. When faint wisps of smoke rose from the chimneys, Marchien knew her father was milking the cows, her mother stirring soup in the pot.

25

III

Even as the dreary days slid into weeks, Marchien refused to give up hope. Someone from the village must find her soon—her father or perhaps Rieks. At thought of the youth, Marchien's heart sank. He'd search everywhere else, not on the heath. *He'd* always called their elders' warning about giants "old wives' tales." And as for her father, perhaps he'd stay away from the heath, along with other village men. He'd think only strangers wandered there—never his daughter!

Marchien had time to ponder these things as she went about her daily tasks. Though she cooked and mended and scrubbed for her captors from morning to night, she was sure that sometime, somehow, she'd get away.

There were days when Marchien fell to brooding about her escape. At first, when they saw the fierce glint in her eyes, the giants chained her to a post. When they decided they'd get more work out of the girl if she were loose, they watched her with lynx eyes. Father and son never hunted together. They never left her alone in the hut. They slept by turns beside the door, while Marchien tossed on a pallet at the rear of the hovel. Neither day nor night did the giants leave the girl unguarded.

Marchien didn't complain. She didn't weep, or talk back, for she was biding her time. But no matter how she tried to please her masters, all she got for her pains were: "Here, clean my boots. And mind you don't spare the oil." "See you don't burn our stew tonight," or "Mend this jacket sleeve, only take care the stitches hold, this time."

For all their threats and roarings, their railings and roughness, the giants never harmed Marchien. Secretly they rejoiced in her, their choicest possession. Behind her back they smacked their lips over her tasty cooking. They were proud when she combed their wild locks. "How did we ever stomach that raw fish and game?" Brammert often asked, when he sniffed the savory stew bubbling on the hearth. "Ha," Ellert would answer, grinning broadly. "So you like our housekeeper, too! Two lone men never fared better than we—but mind the girl never hears *that!*"

As summer passed, the red heather faded and died on the heath. When deep snowdrifts buried the ground as far as Marchien could see, she resigned herself to waiting for spring. No one would be able to get to her till then, she thought.

26

Then at last the snow melted. The heather turned green, buds appeared on the branches. The day the blossoms glowed red in the sun Marchien knew she had been the giants' prisoner a year. That night, the girl shook with stifled sobs. In the morning, she looked toward the village, praying for help.

But as the first year passed, so the second, then the third dragged to an end. "The girl will try to escape us," Ellert whispered one day to his son. "I see that look in her eyes."

"Yes—but just let her try it," cried Brammert, fingering his club.

Three years lengthened into seven. Still Marchien found no way to escape her captors. She no longer had rosy cheeks. The shine had vanished from her yellow hair. From a little distance her faded braids looked almost white. Marchien's shoulders sagged like an old woman's, from lifting the giants' huge pots. Her hands wore torn and stained from scrubbing the hearth and raking ashes. Yet fierce fires still smoldered in the girl's blue eyes. No one will ever come for me now, Marchien finally admitted to herself. I'm going to escape, no matter what happens. If I'm caught it means death, but I'd sooner die than go on living as a slave to these giants!

In spite of her resolve to break away, Marchien had no chance —at least, not until the day that Brammert went hunting in the forest beyond the heath. The old giant, left alone with the girl, decided to have his shave. He stepped outside the hovel to dig a sand hollow where he could sprawl at ease. Marchien bent over the ashes on the hearth.

"Hurry up, girl of Orvelterveen," Ellert bawled after a few moments. "Must I wait all day for you to shave me?"

"I must fill the pot and boil the water," Marchien called from inside the hut. She muttered under her breath, "And how I'd like to boil *you!*"

"Make it quick, then," Ellert roared from the hollow, where he now lolled full length, his head against a pillow of sand. It's a good life, the giant thought, smiling—to be shaved every day by an obedient slave! But to Marchien he rasped, "*I'm* ready. See that razor's sharp enough today not to rip my skin!"

"I'm sharpening the blade now," the girl replied, whetting the steel on the stone until the edge was paper-thin. It's sharp enough to slit your wicked throat, thought Marchien.

"Mind the blade's sharper than yesterday, or I'll beat you so you

27

writhe like a worm," yelled Ellert menacingly. "And aren't you ready *yet?*" he added in a furious tone, though he was grinning.

"In a minute," Marchien called back. "I'm making the lather now." As she swished the stiff brush in the heavy foam, the girl was gazing across the heath toward Orvelterveen. "I'm coming, Mother, Father! *I'm coming!*" she whispered, as a desperate resolve formed in her mind. I may never have such a good chance again, she thought. Brammert is far away in the forest by now.

Marchien lathered the giant's bristly beard until suds billowed over his leathery face like the white fleecy clouds in the sky. She tilted Ellert's head back against the sand until his chin jutted into the air. All the while she was working, the giant hurled bitter complaints. The water was hot enough to boil him, he snarled. Such clumsy hands he'd never seen! Hadn't she learned how to lather him in seven years? *Ouch!* Now she'd slopped soap in his eyes!

Soap! That's it, Marchien thought wildly. She'd blind him with soap, then run away. The girl's hand was steady as she lifted the razor. The long sharp blade glinted in the sun. Marchien crunched through the stubble on the giant's cheek. He was watching her as she moved the blade back and forth expertly. When her little finger accidentally tickled Ellert's nose, he gave a twitch.

"Keep still, you fool," Marchien cried. "This blade is *sharp!*" When she saw a sudden look of terror in the giant's eyes, she brandished the razor above his head as if she intended to cut it open. With her free hand Marchien seized Ellert's beaked nose. She tweaked it and squeezed it until the giant's eyes rolled with fright. He sputtered and huffed, but with that razor blade waving so close, he didn't dare grab the girl.

It's now or never, Marchien thought desperately. Still pinching Ellert's nose, she cast the razor into the sand, where it stuck, the sharp blade pointing up straight. Then the girl snatched at the shaving bowl. Using all her strength, she hurled its hot sudsy contents into the giant's face.

IV

Before Ellert could catch her with his wildly flailing arms, Marchien leaped toward the heath. Then she ran for her life. Behind her the giant, his eyes blinded with soap, smarting with pain, kept yelling, "Come back, come back, girl of Orvelterveen, or I'll kill you. Wait till you taste my club!"

Ellert thrashed to his feet. He groped for the cudgel he'd dropped somewhere. Still unable to see, the giant caught his toe in a heather root. He swayed an instant, then crashed to the ground. He fell face down on the blade that projected like a sword from the sand.

The heath trembled and shook with the terrific force of the giant's fall. When Marchien glanced back she saw Ellert floundering in a pool of blood. His shrieks cut the air. "Brammert, come. I'm dying —dying. Avenge me—*the girl*—"

Marchien covered her ears with her hands. "Dear Heaven, help me," she sobbed. "If Brammert hears—if he comes after me—all is lost."

The girl stumbled on. Then she ran and ran. Desperation gave her limbs new strength. Each step brought her closer to Orvelterveen. In the wild hope that surged through her breast, Marchien forgot the bells, the web at the edge of the heath. All she thought of were father, mother, *home*, as she glimpsed her parents' rye fields, the curly red tiles on their roof. Safety, freedom, were beyond the heath!

At last Marchien sank down on a stone. She must catch her breath, rest a second, before she plunged on. The girl was still panting when she heard Brammert's roar. "You'll pay for it! You'll pay for my father's death, girl of Orvelterveen. I'll spill your blood for his. Just wait till I find you!"

Brammert's bellows came from somewhere near the hut. Marchien jumped to her feet. She darted on blindly. But in her headlong flight, the girl plunged into the trap of threads. As she fell on her face in the intricate web, all the bells clashed at once. They clapped and crashed in such frenzied uproar that Brammert knew where to find his victim.

Marchien's blood froze in her veins when she heard Brammert's voice above the clamor and din of the bells. "*Now* I'll find you. You'll never escape."

As Marchien struggled to get out of the web, she heard Brammert clip-clopping closer and closer. She even heard his heaving gasps. It was then she discovered that the hard work of the past seven years, and her desperation, gave her strength. She tore through the threads. As she leaped from the heath, Brammert was scarcely four rods away.

29

"Revenge, revenge," the giant roared, waving an ax over his head. "You'll never get away from me."

Marchien darted for her father's house. "Father, Father, open the door," she screamed. "The giant's after me with an ax!"

To the girl's horror, the door didn't open. No one was home. Brammert was just reaching out to clutch her flying hair, when a gust of wind swept through the village. The door flew open. Marchien rushed inside. With her last ounce of strength, she slammed the door in Brammert's face. She slipped the heavy bolt through the lock before she fell in a faint.

How long she lay there, Marchien had no notion. But when she finally crawled to her feet, she saw where the giant's ax had crashed against the door—at the exact height of her head! Only the heavy iron hasps inside the door had kept Brammert from breaking through.

That night there was great rejoicing in Orvelterveen, when Marchien's father and mother and all the neighbors returned from a horse fair in a neighboring village. When they found the girl, their gladness knew no end.

"It's a miracle," the old folk murmured. "No one ever came back from Ellert's Field."

In shame the girls and youths hung their heads. They'd never scoff at their elders again!

Marchien's parents held the girl in their arms. Rieks held her hand. "I looked everywhere," he whispered, "*except* in Ellert's Field. I never thought you dead. I never gave up searching, but I didn't believe those giant stories."

"I didn't either," Marchien said.

The villagers clucked in sorrow when they gazed at Marchien's haggard face, her toil-worn hands, the hair that looked white. They shuddered at her account of life as the giants' slave.

"Our rosy darling," they sobbed. "To come to this! We'll feed her, we'll love her back to her old self."

That night the villagers held a feast for Marchien, "the girl who'd returned from the dead." For her, seven bitter years rolled away in a night, as she ate and sang and danced with Rieks.

But while Orvelterveen toasted Marchien, Brammert—back on the heath—was muttering vengeance and death. "I'll teach that wretched girl to trifle with Ellert and Brammert!" he raged, shaking his fist at the village. "I'll destroy her—her family—*everyone*! When I'm through, my father's death will be avenged."

Rumbling with hate and fury, Brammert lay down behind a sandhill. He took a tremendous breath. Then he puffed his great cheeks bigger and bigger. When they looked like two huge red balloons, Brammert started to blow.

He blew sand from the hill toward the village of Orvelterveen. He blew and he blew, until a fine layer of sand covered the rye fields, the roofs of the cottages, the church belfry.

For seven days and seven nights, for seven weeks and seven months, Brammert blew sand. When the villagers saw the storm coming, they fled from their houses to safety in another hamlet.

But Brammert was so busy puffing out clouds of sand, he never knew his victims had escaped.

When the giant had done with his blowing, he stiffly rose to his feet. The village was a desert, a desolate sand pile no living creature could survive.

"This is my revenge, girl of Orvelterveen," Brammert roared. "People shall call yonder mound *Brammertshoop*, Brammert's Heap, to the end of time."

Though the giants have disappeared from northeastern Holland, people still point to Ellertsveld as the loneliest, the largest and the loveliest heath in mooi Drenthe. And they still show strangers Brammertshoop, the sandhill that entombs the lost village of Orvelterveen.

3

THE DEERHURST WORM
(England)

Long ago, in the days of the Saxons, a monster once pillaged Deerhurst, a peaceful hamlet on the banks of the Severn. Of the many fearsome monsters that plagued England's West Country, this one was most fearsome of all. He was so savage he starved the farmers, so long his body reached around the village three times.

Since the dreadful creature flourished centuries ago, the people of Deerhurst do not remember whether he was dragon, serpent or beast. It's the Vicar, who knows more about long-ago things than most folks know about today, who thinks he was a Worm.

"An extraordinary monster of prodigious bigness," he told me. "Around his neck were long tight scales no sword could penetrate. Tough hide covered his body, to the tip of his tail. And as to his head —*that was the head of a beast*! Yet he was a worm. Quite definitely, yes."

To prove he was right, the Vicar pointed to a hideous gargoyle that leered from the tower of the Priory Church. The cold stone eyes stared toward the valley. The small ears stood alert to whisk of beetle, or whirr of wing. The lapping lips were cruel.

"A Saxon craftsman who'd once *seen* the Worm carved his image in stone," the Vicar went on. "Then he placed the head in the west face of the tower. There the monster has remained—more than nine hundred years—to warn other marauders of the Deerhurst Worm's fate."

Though it's hard to say after so many years just how the Worm reached Deerhurst, we *think* it happened one moonlit night in May. For three days and three nights the monster had swum the Severn in frantic flight from his foe, the Witch of Wales. She scudded after him on her broomstick, above the riverbank. "I'll get you yet, you sneaking Worm," she howled, flapping her wand at his tail. "No thief can slither into *my* brew, then swim away alive."

The Worm didn't answer, for his strength was rapidly ebbing. I'm lost if the old hag touches me, he thought. He tried in vain to move faster. But the Worm's tired body sagged. He gasped for air. Each breath was pain. The witch was gaining, inch by inch. "Ha," she screamed, so close the Worm jumped. "I'll smack you soon. *Then* you'll wish you hadn't snooped!"

As his pursuer's wand whizzed through the air, the Worm remembered in time that *witches can't cross water!* The Worm lurched toward the far side of the Severn where, though he didn't know it, the village of Deerhurst nestled among the trees. He managed to clamber up the banks just as the witch smote the water a terrible blow.

The Worm lay panting among the reeds. When he opened his eyes, he heard a clock striking midnight from the tower of a church. Bright moonlight streamed across the rolling pasture lands, where sheep and cows lay sleeping. The hideous howls of the witch had ceased. Slowly the Worm reared his head. There wasn't a sound, save nightingales singing in a copse.

"This is where I'll make my home," the Worm declared, stretching stiffly. The Witch of Wales can never reach me here."

At thought of the witch, the Worm chortled. "No wonder she chased me," he cried, as he slithered through the high wet grass toward a clump of oaks on Walton Hill. "*I* heard her spell, before I lapped her brew to the last bitter drop.

> " 'Toad's eye,
> Tooth of fox,
> Snail's horn,
> Black cat's whisker.
> Whoever drinks this magic potion
> Men shall remember a thousand years.' "

Still gloating, the Worm crawled up the hill. Near the top, he found a cool hollow. "This shall be my lair," he cried, coiling for a nap. "Under these oaks, beside this pool, I'll lead the life of a robber baron. From here I can see the entire valley. I'll plunder and rob it at will."

From the night the Worm came to Deerhurst, the inhabitants lived in terror. At first no one knew *who* milked the cows before dawn,

33

who stole butter and cream, *who* sucked the hens' eggs, leaving empty shells in the nests.

As things went from bad to worse, each man eyed his neighbor with mistrust. Farmers set traps in the pastures. They watched their barns behind closed shutters. Yet for all their spying no one could discover the thief. For the Worm could wriggle through clovers and grasses without anyone seeing his long slim body. With each passing day, the people grew leaner while the Worm grew fatter. When the children fretted with hunger, their elders ground their teeth.

"What's going on here?" farmers demanded, when they met at the Bull tavern to discuss their problem. "We'll skin the hide off the rascal's back—*once we find him,*" they yelled, banging down their mugs at the tavern.

When the Worm heard the farmers' threats, he slapped his fat sides with his tail. "Fools! Idiots!" he snortled, rocking in glee beside the pool. "I slink through the meadow under their noses—yet no one sees me!" Still chuckling, the Worm slid up an oak. He looped his body in and out of the branches. "If one of those chickenhearted louts ever saw me," he yawned, "he'd drop dead of fright."

The sun shone brightly as the Worm settled for sleep. His head nodded over a limb of the tree. By the time he was dozing, his nose almost touched the ground. The long, sleek scales that fitted his neck like a collar billowed out in a ruff, leaving the tender part of his neck exposed, for the Worm felt safe enough.

While the monster was dreaming of the milk and cream he'd steal that night, Nab Smith, the blacksmith's young son, was climbing the hill with his blackberry basket. "The best blackberries grew around the pond last year," the small boy told a toad in the grass. "Our mam's promised a tart, if I find the blackberries."

Even *they* were scarce this year, Nab reflected, as he stared at the sour shriveled pips in his basket. Someone had almost stripped the bushes. Yet *who?* the lad wondered. Nobody he knew had blackberries this year. It must be that thief everybody talked about, everywhere in Deerhurst.

Nab plodded on up the hill. Then he stopped as though rooted in the grass. He shook with terror. Gooseflesh rose all over his body. From up in the oaks came a horrible grating—*hurr-ha, hurr-ha, hurr-rr-r.* The noise sounded again and again. It was as regular and loud as the whirr of the grinding wheel Nab's father had in his shop.

It's a lion or maybe a bear, thought the lad, still too frightened to move. He peered about frantically—at the pond, the rocks, the trees. *Then Nab saw the Worm*, who was hanging upside down in the oak. The rhythmic *hurrings* came from the creature's wide-open mouth!

With a loud scream Nab pelted down the hill. He spilled his basket of blackberries. He didn't pause for breath. He didn't look behind. He ran straight to his father, who was shoeing a horse in his smithy. The boy fell into his father's arms, sobbing wildly.

As John Smith, the burly young blacksmith, held his shivering son, he said, "Come, come, Nab, let's dry those tears. Tell me what's the matter."

A bit at a time, the boy blurted out his adventure on the hill. "I saw him—I saw him, a d-d-dreadful Worm. He had a r-ruff around his neck," Nab cried through teeth that chattered. "He was snoring so loudly he never s-stopped, even when I screamed."

"And lucky for you he didn't!" John Smith said, hugging Nab close. Just then Will Turner came back for his horse. The blacksmith sent the lad home to his mother with the warning, "Don't go black-berrying again."

When the two men were alone, John Smith repeated the boy's story. "Now, at least, we know who is ravaging the countryside. The next thing's to decide what to do."

When the Worm found Nab's basket and the scattered black-berries on the side of the hill, he hissed in fury. "So, someone spied upon me while I slept! Someone's seen my lair. I'll teach the snooper a lesson." Then the Worm growled so loudly the farmers thought a storm was coming on.

That night the Worm's plunderings were worse than ever. He spit venom at the river until the eels died. He plowed up fields with his tail. As time went on and the villagers tried to track the monster down, his meanness increased. People even talked of leaving Deerhurst. "But where can we go?" they cried.

When at last the inhabitants could bear no more, they addressed a petition to the King. "Send help," they pleaded. "Send a brave warrior to slay the Worm whose lair is on Walton Hill. Our village is dying. Soon *we* shall be dead."

The King was so moved by the villagers' plight that he paced the floor night and day. "But what can I do?" he cried in despair.

"The foreign foe presses at the gate. I can spare no good knight to help Deerhurst. *The men of the village must help themselves.*"

The King speedily dispatched a herald to the stricken hamlet. As the horseman clattered into the green, he blew on his silver horn. "Hear ye! Hear ye!" he shouted. "I bring a message from His Royal Highness, the King."

The inhabitants hurried to the green from cottage and field. They gathered around the herald and his foaming horse. They watched him break the seal on the parchment scroll in his hand. Then they listened as the messenger read a proclamation that ended:

"His Majesty begs you, valiant men of Deerhurst, to do battle at once with the Worm. You alone must find the way to destroy the monster. As the peril is great, so also is the prize. Upon the brave victor, and his descendants the King of the realm will bestow his Crown estates on Walton Hill."

His message delivered, the herald spurred his horse. Then he sped from the village in a cloud of dust. The inhabitants of Deerhurst stared after the rider, too awed to speak. At last an old man cackled, "Walton Hill—everyone knows, even the Worm—that's the finest parcel of land for miles about."

"Aye, it's a royal prize the King offers," a farmer agreed, pulling at his beard.

"Any woman would be happy to make a home there," a toil-worn wife said wistfully. "Her man would be a yeoman."

"Who knows, perhaps even a knight with a plume in his hat!" a young bride murmured.

After the men had sent their wives home to mind the children, they settled down at the Bull to discuss the King's proclamation.

"Now we're back where we started," grumbled Tim Eagles, gulping his ale. "What we want is *help*, not fancy promises. As if we hadn't done all we could already!"

"Or liked hearing our babies cry for milk," sighed a father of three.

"Or seeing our pretty girls skinny and pale," a youth mumbled.

When Fox Freeman complained, "What good are Crown lands if a man lose his life?" young John Smith stormed to the door of the tavern. "We'll *all* lose our lives," he shouted, "if we don't do something besides talk."

"Well, why don't *you*, then?" sneered Ron Rymer.

The men were still talking as John Smith strode toward his smithy. His black eyes snapped with anger as he tied his leather apron around his waist. He picked up his hammer. *He* had no time to waste, though others did. With seven mouths to feed, life wasn't easy, even in good times. And now, with the Worm pilfering butter, and stealing milk from Buttercup, their one cow, John's children went to bed hungry five nights out of seven. Then there was Nab. He'd been ailing, since his fright on the hill.

John sighed deeply as he began hammering a horseshoe. How he wished things were easier for his wife, Lizzie. The blacksmith's rhythmic blows sang through the village. Lizzie made-do and mended, stretched out the soup—yet she always had smiles for him and the children. She's one girl in a million, the young man thought warmly. He'd like to see *her* in a place on Walton Hill, not the old cottage with leaky thatch!

As he hit ferocious blows with his hammer, John muttered between clenched teeth, "I wish *this* were the head of the Worm!" He kept thinking how often he'd crept up the hill with his hammer, hoping to knock the Worm's block off. Yet he'd never been able to find the monster. John hadn't even *seen* the creature, though he didn't doubt Nab's story—not for a minute.

While his hammer rose and fell as though life depended on the racket he made, John had an idea. It was so tremendous he threw down his hammer with a clatter. Then the blacksmith guffawed until the dingy rafters shook.

"It's a trap so simple, so sure to succeed," he cried. "Why didn't I think of what Nab said about the Worm's ruff? All I need is patience, and a bucket of milk." John's ruddy face fell at thought of how little the Worm left Buttercup nowadays.

Without squandering precious time on *ifs* and *ands*, John lifted a long-handled ax from a peg on the wall. Gingerly he tested the blade. "Ouch!" he grunted, sucking the blood that spurted from his thumb. "The edge is fine!"

John's eyes danced with excitement as he strapped the ax to his shoulder. He snatched up a bucket, then ran to the pasture where Buttercup was chewing her cud. She stared at her master as he strode toward her, then tossed her pretty head.

"Everything depends on you, my beauty," John cried, affectionately rubbing Buttercup's nose. Then he set down the bucket and started to milk. At first he thought there wouldn't be enough to even half fill the pail. But as John squeezed the udder, the rich stream flowed faster. It stopped just when it reached the bucket's rim.

"Well done," cried John, kissing the star on Buttercup's forehead. "If I win the prize, you'll be queen o' my herd," he said gaily as he started toward Walton Hill.

Buttercup mooed as if she'd understood. John cautiously climbed toward the oaks. The Worm might be *anywhere*, he thought as he crept from one grassy hump to another. He hid behind rocks. He crouched under hedgerows. Once John stubbed his toe. Steady, boy, he told himself. If I spill this milk, like as not the Worm will spill my blood.

When he neared the hollow where the Worm had his lair, John stopped to listen. There wasn't a sound, except the crickets fiddling in the grass, a lone robin trilling in a bush. There was no sign of the Worm. John set his bucket down in a small clearing near the hollow. Then he slid behind the trunk of a tree.

After what seemed a lifetime, John heard swishings and slidings in the meadow. When he saw a fearsome head rising, not three rods away, he thought frantically, He's coming at me! But the Worm only sniffed. Then he darted for the pail, gurgling with joy.

Slurp—slurp—slurp. The Worm's long red tongue lapped around and around inside the pail, until not one drop of milk remained. For a long time the monster lay still in the sun. Then he gradually pulled his great length into the tree overhead.

"I fancy those farmers aren't so stupid as they seem," the Worm said, with a tremendous yawn. "Whoever saw me asleep the other day knew what I liked. Now, if they'd *all* bring milk here, I'd steal less."

By now the Worm's eyes were so heavy he had trouble looping his body through the limbs of the tree. He started to doze. Little by little, his head drooped toward the ground. When the Worm hung motionless, upside down, John saw the close scales around the neck slowly unfold. That's the ruff Nab talked about, the blacksmith thought. He held the ax so tightly his hand ached.

John didn't dare stir until he heard the steady *hurr-ha, hurr-ha, hurr* from the Worm's mouth. Only then did the blacksmith creep from behind the tree, one step at a time. When close to the Worm, John took a deep breath. He raised the ax above his head. Then he smashed the blade down on the monster's neck.

The blow was so savage, so powerful, so sudden, that the Worm's head bounced off like a rubber ball. But before John had a chance to dodge it, the tail lashed at him. It swept the blacksmith from his feet. Then it flogged him until he rolled in the grass.

The thrashings of the Worm's tail made the earth shake until the men rushed from the Bull to see what was amiss. When they found John sprawled on the hillside, he was too dazed to speak. At last he opened his eyes. He stared stupidly at the anxious faces about him. Then he asked, "What's the matter?"

"*Nothing*," Will Turner whooped. "You've killed the Worm!"

"Aye," said Ron Rymer with a sheepish grin. "While we *talked* about the Worm over cheese and ale, you won the prize."

With cheers and shouts the men took John home. The lads spiked the beast to a pole. They marched away, chanting:

"The Worm, the Worm,
He's dead, dead, dead.
Come out and see
His dreadful head."

The villagers streamed from their cottages to find out what was going on. When Lizzie caught sight of her man's bloody face, she sobbed in his arms as if her heart would break.

"He's a hero," the others shouted, crowding around the couple.

"It's all over," John whispered in Lizzie's ear. "Dry your tears, my dear. Nab is coming. *He's* the hero!" The blacksmith swung the boy to his shoulder. "*He* saw the Worm first. But for Nabbie—and Buttercup—the Worm would be robbing us yet."

When the King heard how a blacksmith had killed the Worm with a pail of milk and an ax, he laughed until tears ran down his cheeks. "John Smith is the kind of man this country needs," he declared. "He *belongs* on our Crown lands."

John and Lizzie, their five children, and *their* children's children, lived in a fine house the King had built on Walton Hill. And as for Buttercup—the day the King heard about *her*, he ordered a barn to house her, and sent a herd of yellow cows to keep her company.

It's going on a thousand years now since the Worm ravaged Deerhurst, the village on the Severn. Yet he is still remembered—just as the witch promised in her spell.

4

THE LAST STONE

(France: Pays Basque)

In southern France, on the western slope of the Pyrenees near the Spanish border, lies the beautiful French Pays Basque. The Basques are a race apart, for no one knows whence they came. *Eskuara*, the tongue they speak, is so hard to learn that Basques tell you it's the language of heaven!

The Pays Basque is a mysterious land. Devils, demons and witches roam the high mountains. And beneath rushing waters, in rivers and gorges, the hairy *Laminak* live. Nowadays one seldom sees these monsters, who look like little old men. But long, long ago, when Ramuntcho was Seigneur of Laustania Château, sensible folk crossed themselves when anyone mentioned the creatures by name.

Now, young Ramuntcho had never believed such monsters existed—not until that cold windy night when he met one in the great hall of his château.

The seigneur's adventure started when he sat alone, booding beside the fire. With unseeing eyes he stared at his family's proud arms carved in the stones over the fireplace. He listened to the wind howling around the broken chimneys outside. He watched the threadbare tapestries billow out, in sudden blasts of air that whipped through chinks in the broken masonry.

"Those lovely ladies on their snow-white palfreys, those plumed knights stalking red deer," Ramuntcho muttered, gazing at the faded tatters with melancholy eyes. "I wonder what they'd say if they could see themselves now, hanging in rags on these moldering walls."

In spite of the cloak Ramuntcho held about his shoulders, he shivered with cold. As the dying embers clinked to the hearth, one by one, the youth buried his face in his hands.

"It's all over," Ramuntcho groaned. "I've lost her—lost my lovely Graciane forever. On Sunday her father will wed her to rich old Fermin—because I've discovered no hidden hoard of gold!"

41

Ramuntcho thought bitterly of his argument with Graciane's peasant father, a twelfthmonth ago. He remembered every word, the night he asked for Graciane's hand.

"And what can *you* offer, aside from high birth?" the insolent old man taunted. "A tumbledown château high above a gorge, a wheezing old woman to cook the meals! Why, if my Graciane married you, she'd work her pretty fingers to the bone. With her beauty, my daughter can marry Fermin. He's rich, though so old he'll soon be dead. He'll give her a horse and carriage, servants to do her bidding, silks and satins as befit a fine lady. Tell me, boy, what can you do?"

"I can give Graciane *love*," Ramuntcho cried, drawing himself up proudly. "I can give her a noble name, and a house that has sheltered kings in its time. Graciane and I have grown up together. She's never looked at another youth. I have no money, but I have two strong hands, and a love for my father's land."

"Strong hands, bah! What you need is money," the grasping peasant exclaimed. A cunning smile twisted his lips and he leaned closer to Ramuntcho. "Your father, the old seigneur, folk say was rich. Has he left you, his only son, *nothing*?"

"Nothing," Ramuntcho admitted, "except his title, his château and his debts."

Graciane's father hitched his chair closer and studied the youth's face with greedy eyes. Then he poured out two glasses of wine. "I'm a reasonable father," the old man continued, offering a glass to the youth. "You'd make Graciane a good husband, provided you had something besides love to offer. You're both young. Perhaps you'll find something—some hidden wealth, some hoard your father has left you. *I* know the seigneur had it! Where could it have gone? He must have hidden it, for some strange reason of his own."

The peasant refilled their glasses before he went on. "I'll give you a year from today to find the treasure, and to rebuild your old château so it's as grand as it was before you were born. Love will find a way," he added, with a sly wink at the young man. "But if it doesn't, Graciane shall marry Fermin. It's a bad father who doesn't look out for his daughter!"

"I tell you, my father left no hidden treasure," Ramuntcho said in disgust. "It's useless to hunt for what isn't there!"

Ramuntcho groaned again as he thought how he had toiled

during the past months to make the old château fit for his bride. But with only two hands, and no money, how much could he do? The ancient roof still leaked like a sieve. The stones were crumbling with age.

"I'd need enough gold to fill a dozen coffers to restore this ancestral place to its former glory," the youth exclaimed. "Alas, everything's over for Graciane and me. She's crying her pretty eyes out this minute because her father won't let her wed me, and my heart is well nigh unto breaking. In two days, the time her father gave me will be up."

Ramuntcho's fingers closed on the dagger at his belt, as he tried to imagine life without the girl he loved. "If I can't have you, my darling," he cried, "there's nothing left for me—though I'd give my soul to win you, my Graciane."

Ramuntcho stared into space, too miserable to notice the soot and rubble that suddenly tumbled from the chimney, too lost in melancholy to hear stealthy pad-paddings on the stone floor. He startedly violently when a high voice squeaked in his ear.

"*Would* you, Ramuntcho? Would you give your soul to win Graciane?"

I'm dreaming, the youth thought. There's no one here. But as he turned quickly in the direction of the voice, he found himself gazing into two pale, round, marblelike eyes. They belonged to a small hairy creature, with pointed ears and a pointed gray beard. Standing at Ramuntcho's elbow, the creature regarded him without blinking.

"W-wh-who are you?" gasped Ramuntcho, too startled to move.

"Don't be afraid," the stranger shrilled, advancing a step. "I'm Guillen, a Lamina—one of the little men. I won't hurt you. I was hiding in the chimney. When I heard what you said, I slid down the flue to offer my help."

"*Help*," repeated Ramuntcho dully. "No one can help me now."

"That's where you're wrong!" shouted Guillen, jumping up and down in glee. For the first time Ramuntcho noticed that his strange caller wore no clothes—only thick shaggy hair on arms, legs and the stubby body with the bulging stomach. Still staring into the young man's eyes, the little monster stepped closer.

"Listen," he said. "Tomorrow, between nightfall and the first cockcrow, I and my fellows can rebuild this Château. We'll fetch pink marble from the gorge. We'll cut the stones, polish them until they shine. Then we'll lay the blocks, end on end. We'll bind them with mortar to last a thousand years. Before the first cock crows at midnight, the Château of Laustania shall rise anew—more glorious than in the day of your sires. In addition to restoring the château, we'll give you a coffer brimming with gold. Then you, Ramuntcho, can claim your bride. You and the beautiful Graciane shall rule this house in honor and wealth to the end of your days."

In spite of himself, Ramuntcho's face flushed with excitement. His brown eyes brightened with hope. The Laminak—he remembered hearing old peasants speak of these small hairy creatures, of the wondrous things they could do. But—there was some catch! As he groped to recall what it was, he studied Guillen's grinning face.

"You and your companions can perform such miracles?" Ramuntscho asked. "*You* can rebuild the château in a single night?"

The astonishment in the young man's face delighted Guillen. He leaped into the air with a whoop. Then he pirouetted grotesquely the length of the hall. As the monster whirled away, then started to return, words of his old nurse flashed into Ramuntcho's mind.

"Always beware of Laminak," she had warned him as a boy. "They are monsters—creatures of darkness—who offer their help to men. The Laminak dwell deep down beneath black waters of river and sea. When darkness falls they come from hiding. By moonlight they ride through the sky, astride great horned owls. Though the Laminak can perform great wonders for men, the price they demand is dear."

Ramuntcho was thinking of these words as Guillen bounded toward him, chanting:

"By moonlight we'll do it, do it,
We'll do it by moonlight.
We'll rebuild the house of your fathers
For you, for lovely Graciane.
To the seigneur we'll give
Riches and glory in life,
And then—and then—"

" 'And then—' " shouted Ramuntcho. "Then—*what*? Name your price."

"We'll claim your soul," replied the Lamina in a matter-of-fact voice. "A small price, I must say, for a bride like Graciane," he added as Ramuntcho blanched. "All you have to do is sign an agreement in your own blood. It's all quite simple. We won't bother you as long as you live, but when you die—"

"When I die?" quavered Ramuntcho, shaking so he could hardly speak.

"When you die, we'll carry away your soul, of course," said Guillen with a harsh laugh. "Unless—"

"Unless what?" Ramuntcho cried, springing from his chair. "And how do I know you'll keep your part of the bargain if I do consent to this pact?"

"We'll start building at dusk, tomorrow night," said Guillen. "If we *haven't* finished—to the last stone—before the first cockcrow, the place will be yours, and you'll be free of your bargain. We'll vanish forever. But if we *do* complete our task before the first cockcrow," Guillen added, shaking with mirth, "you'd best remember, young man, your soul will be ours."

Ramuntcho's blood chilled at the evil he saw in the pale eyes. He stood before the hearth without speaking. Then he glanced at the worm-eaten beams, the crumbling walls, the holes through which the wind whistled. After all, I've nothing to lose, he thought, fingering his dagger again. Without Graciane I can't live. By signing my soul away, I can have her.

At thought of the girl, the warm blood raced through Ramuntcho's veins, courage came to his heart. If he signed the pact now, he might think of a way to outwit the monsters before cockcrow tomorrow. And if he didn't he'd have Graciane.

Pondering thus, Ramuntcho turned to Guillen, whose cold eyes still watched him. "I'll sign the agreement," said the youth. Rolling his sleeve back, he pricked his forearm with the point of his dagger. When red blood spurted out, Ramuntcho seized a quill pen from the table. Dipping the point into the blood on his arm, he wrote these words on a scrap of parchment:

I, Ramuntcho, Seigneur of Laustania Château, do hereby agree to give my soul to the Laminak when I die—provided they rebuild my château before the first cockcrow tomorrow.

46

Ramuntcho dated the agreement. He signed his name in a firm hand, then tossed the document to Guillen. With a howl of triumph the Lamina snatched it.

"Until tomorrow," Ramuntcho said shortly.

"Until tomorrow," shrieked Guillen, leaping toward the hearth. He whooshed up the chimney with a yell. Outside, Ramuntcho heard the wind moan like a dying beast. The great hall echoed with the monster's cries.

Alone once more, Ramuntcho paced the floor with heavy steps. Troubled thoughts spun in his head. The clock in the tower was striking three, the candles sputtering, when the youth exclaimed, "Dear Heaven, help me—before it's too late—to think of a way to thwart the monsters."

Before throwing himself on his bed, Ramuntcho peered toward the valley where Graciane lived with her father. "Don't weep, my darling," he whispered softly. "Things will come right. You're going to wed *me*, not Fermin. I'll send old Mayi with a message as soon as I can. I'll think of something. And if I don't, we shall be happy—as long as possible."

After restless tossings and troubled dreams, Ramuntcho rose to milk the cows and feed the pigs. He tried to whistle, but his lips were dry. He kept saying, "Tomorrow—Sunday—Graciane will be my bride." But in spite of his joy, his hands were clammy with dread. He still hadn't thought how to outwit the Laminak.

Ramuntcho was so distracted that he stumbled on a stone in the barnyard. When he leaned over to cast it from his path, Roujain, the youngest cock, flapped to his shoulder. There the rooster perched, regarding his master from beady black eyes. As Ramuntcho reached out his hand to caress the shining red-gold feathers, he suddenly threw back his head and laughed.

"Roujain," Ramuntcho shouted, hugging the cock, "you're a clever bird! You've just told me what I must do. It's a sign! Together, you and I can outwit the monsters!"

Setting the cock down with a pat, Ramuntcho rushed toward the courtyard. There Mayi, the old servingwoman, was turning flax in the sun.

"Mayi, Mayi," he called. "I want you to go to the valley. Tell

Graciane all is well. Tell her to dry her tears. Tomorrow she'll marry *me!*"

"*You!*" wheezed the old woman, touching Ramuntcho's flushed face. "Are you sick, or out of your senses?"

"That I'm not," laughed Ramuntcho, hugging the old woman affectionately. "Now hurry," he ordered, fetching Mayi's stick. "And mind you keep out of the old man's way. His heart's set on Fermin, and his horse and carriage, for Graciane!"

"*That* one!" sniffed Mayi, as she hobbled toward the village.

When the old woman turned the bend in the road, Ramuntcho rushed back to the flax. He snatched it by handfuls. Then he stuffed it inside his shirt—until his chest bulged like a turkey's.

"There, that ought to do it!" Ramuntcho cried, patting the bulge. "When Mayi returns, she won't know what's happened to her precious flax—or how much I need it."

All day as Ramuntcho worked in the fields, the flax scratched his skin. But he didn't mind. He sang so loudly as he guided the plow that the oxen turned their heads. "We'll win, we'll win," the youth chanted, thinking of his darling Graciane.

At dusk Ramuntcho ran toward the henhouse, a stick in his hand. It won't be long before the Laminak come, he thought, watching evening gather over the valley. He could still see the church tower, the red tiles of Graciane's roof, as he mounted the henhouse ladder. He peered inside at the shadowy forms of the hens and cocks huddled on their perches, heads under wings. He counted the birds once, then twice—to be sure all were there. In his favorite place beside the door, Roujain roosted as usual. Ramuntcho laughed softly, fingering the flax at his bosom. Then he sat down on the top round of the ladder to wait.

It wasn't long before Ramuntcho heard voices from the gorge rising shrilly above the rushing river. Then he saw them—hundreds and hundreds of shaggy gray heads, bobbing up from the water. It's the Laminak! They're here, the youth thought, his heart bumping until he thought it would rouse the hens. Then he saw Guillen leap to a rock. He beckoned the other Laminak to follow him.

The little man stood, feet wide apart, arms swinging like windmills. Ramuntcho could tell he was directing his companions to *go yonder, do that.* The youth saw the monsters dash here and there.

48

Then they propped a long ladder against the cliff. They clambered up like monkeys. Soon they set up a second ladder, against the crumbling walls of the château.

As darkness fell, Ramuntcho couldn't *see* what happened next. But he *heard* scramblings and scurryings—often loud grunts—on the ladders. And from the gorge there were bangings of heavy mallets, chipping of stones. Ramuntcho's perch swayed and wove as hundreds of feet pounded toward the top of the château.

From the gorge came muffled voices, then words repeated over and over like a chant.

"Take it, Guillen."

"Catch it, Guillen."

"Pass it on, Guillen."

Soon the moon appeared from behind the clouds. By its bright light Ramuntcho saw Guillen, still standing on the rock. Laminak in the gorge tossed to him huge blocks of pink rock, cut and polished to gleaming perfection. Guillen caught them as lightly as thistledown. Then he hurled them to his fellows on the ladder. Hand over hand, an army of these creatures passed the stones up and up, until they reached the builders astride the château.

In the moonlight Ramuntcho saw the old house grow in glory. Stone by stone the structure mounted toward the sky. Never in the days of his fathers had the walls of the ancient château glowed so richly. Never had the battlements been so strong, the polished turrets so slim.

As Ramuntcho watched the monsters work in frantic haste, he didn't lose track of the time. When the clock in the tower struck ten —then eleven—he clutched at the flax next his breast. He glanced at the moon for the hundredth time. There horned owls hovered with outstretched wings. Minute by minute, the birds floated lower until they hung over the heads of the hairy builders.

"It's almost midnight," Ramuntcho whispered. "The owls are here to carry the Laminak away." From his bosom he snatched out the flax. He wound it round and round his stick, while the owls screamed, *Too-whoo-oo-o.*

From deep in the gorge the rhythmic chant still came.

"Take it, Guillen."

"Catch it, Guillen."

"Pass it, Guillen."

49

It's nearly time now, thought Ramuntcho as he watched the builders drop stone after stone into place. When he saw the last stone coming up the ladder—the one that was meant for the top—the youth lighted his torch. The flax blazed into blinding brightness. Ramuntcho waved the torch outside the henhouse door.

The flare startled Roujain from sleep. He roused with a start. It's the sun, the cock thought in panic. I've overslept! Though still half asleep, the young rooster stretched his neck. He flapped his red-gold wings. Then standing straight and tall, he crowed.

Cock-a-doodle-do! COCK-A-DOODLE-DO-OO!

Louder and louder Roujain crowed, so the sun wouldn't think he'd been caught asleep. The cock finished his crowing as the flare faded. The clock in the tower was striking twelve.

"Wicked cock!" yelled the Laminak, trembling with rage. "Now we're lost—undone!"

The Lamina who held the last stone let it crash from his hands. The block hurtled into the gorge, sweeping hundreds and hundreds of hairy monsters from the ladders. The huge stone smashed into the foaming waters of the ravine with a shattering roar that wakened folk in the valley from sleep.

Ramuntcho saw Guillen alone on the rock. He turned, shaking his fist at the rooster. Then he leaped after his companions, with a wail.

Ramuntcho threw his arms about the young cock—now drooping with shame because he'd mistaken the torch for the sun. "You've done it, you've done it," cried Ramuntcho, planting a kiss on the rooster's red comb. "The monsters have vanished. You've saved me from my pact." As the youth stroked Roujain's feathers, he whispered, "For breakfast, my friend, I'll dig you a potful of worms—and give you an extra measure of corn."

That morning, when Graciane's father rose and gazed out the window toward the château, he thought he'd taken leave of his senses. The battlements, the slender turrets shone rosy pink against the blue of the sky. Instead of a ruined old pile of stones, the château gleamed like a fairy palace.

The old man pinched himself. He stared at the château a second, then a third time. "It's—it's the work of witches," was all he could say.

50

When Graciane's father hurried to the garden to tell his daughter the wonderful news, he found her in Ramuntcho's arms.

"So the seigneur, your father, *was* rich—as I always told you," the old man said, when he got the youth's attention. "You found the hoard, then got witches' help!"

Ramuntcho only grinned. Then he kissed Graciane again. Again he asked her hand. This time the old peasant gladly gave his consent. To be mistress of such a fine château was better, he reasoned, than to wed Fermin with his horse and carriage! And of course the young seigneur would make a rich son. He'd probably found bags and bags of gold!

That day the priest married Ramuntcho and Graciane in the village church. Old Mayi was there in a new cap with ribbons, and so were all the valley folk. Everyone rejoiced in the match, though all marveled at the poor young seigneur's sudden good fortune. Ramuntcho never disclosed to anyone—save the priest and his Graciane—what really happened. He let Graciane's father invent his own version of that!

"Those two always belonged together," the villagers murmured after the wedding. Even old Fermin had to agree, when he saw the young couple's happy faces.

To Ramuntcho and his bride, each day was happier than the one before, in their château with the last stone missing. "That's our luck," the young man always said, pointing to the gorge.

To this day, the great pink stone lies in the river bed where the Lamina builder dropped it, at Roujain's crow.

Roujain, who lived to a ripe old age, always rode about the barnyard on his master's shoulder. Every day Ramuntcho dug seven fat worms for his breakfast, and added an extra measure of corn. "Were it not for Roujain," the seigneur reminded his bride, "Guillen could claim my soul!"

To the end of his days, the Seigneur of Laustania honored his cocks. With loving care he carved a rooster in the family arms over the fireplace of the great hall.

5

THE CANDLE OF DEATH

(Ireland)

Long, long before Brian Boru—Ireland's great tenth-century king—built his fortress on Carrigonnul Rock, the ogress Grana lived there. She was so frightful-looking that even wolves slunk away from her in terror. Her beaked nose was so sharp it could cut down a tree, her long yellow fangs so long they could crush a boar's back.

Grana was a giantess. She was so tall that to see the top of her head, one had to stand on tiptoe and peer toward the sky. The strength of her arm was that of threescore men. Yet it wasn't only Grana's looks—the horrible face, the gigantic body, or even the power of her dreadful hands—that terrorized people most. *It was the evil deep in her heart.* Grana was more wicked than the wickedest demon inside the earth. Death was her pastime. Destruction was her joy.

The ogress ravaged the fair Shannon valley that lay beneath her rock. When she puffed out her shriveled cheeks and blew a hot blast over the fields, corn withered on the stalk. Pastures lay parched and brown. A single glance from her wicked eyes and the cows went dry. Lambs died in the fold.

Such outrages were nothing compared to Grana's sport with the Candle of Death. The candle was bewitched. It was an evil thing. The ogress lighted it each night and placed it on her rock. Any man who gazed upon the flame lay there dead before dawn.

To the unwary, the burning candle was a beacon in the night. The light beckoned to sailors tossing at sea, to men toiling at their nets, to those lost in a storm. Such were the victims Grana drew to their doom.

The ogress always hid in the shadows, waiting for her quarry. "Ha," she shrieked, when she pounced upon her prey. "Another fool has met his death."

The old hag's dreadful laughter echoed like thunder through

the still valley. She howled with glee as she devoured her victim, then hurled his bones, one by one, into the fast-flowing Shannon.

Whenever people heard the horrible noise, they clustered in shivery groups and wondered whom Grana had destroyed, *and whose turn might be next.*

"The Candle of Death has lured another man to his end," women sobbed. "Another mother robbed of her son . . . another wife of her man."

"Aye, aye," husbands answered, trying to keep their voices steady. "Grana has made more orphans tonight. We live in evil times. When will this wickedness cease?"

Thus one awful night followed another. No man could resist the lure of the candle. Even its faintest glimmer dragged him toward it—as surely as a magnet attracts steel. As time went on Grana's laughter grew more raucous. The Candle of Death claimed more men.

At last the stricken people cried, "We are doomed. We have no hope. There is none to help us. All of Erin's wise men are not wise enough to outwit the ogress. All of Erin's soldiers cannot match her strength."

But at the very moment their plight was most desperate, aid came to the folk of the Shannon valley, from far to the east. There Finn, the mighty warrior, defender of High King Cormac's peace, was holding counsel with Erin's soldier brotherhood, the *Fianna.* The men, picked for bold feats of prowess, pressed about their leader as he told them of a robber who had sacked a village and taken the women captive.

"We must punish the marauder," vowed the Fianna men. Their sworn duty was to succor the afflicted, to help the weak throughout the land. Wherever wrongs had to be righted, Finn sent his warriors. A hundred bards recited their deeds. Thrice three hundred grateful hearts sang their praise.

During the tumult that followed Finn's disclosure, a wandering monk hurried into the council chamber.

"I bring grave news," he panted, as soon as he could speak. "I have hastened from the west to tell you of Grana, the ogress, who burns the Candle of Death each night. She ravages the countryside. She is devouring Shannon's men. Already," the monk concluded, "only white-haired grandfathers and beardless youths remain."

53

In fury Finn pounded the council table with his mighty fist. "The old hag must die," he thundered.

Rage and horror gleamed in the eyes of the assembled warriors. Finn searched their faces. Then he roared, "Before another night has fallen, this outrage must cease. One of you must destroy Grana—must destroy her candle forever!"

No man spoke when Finn had finished. In the heavy silence that followed his words, each heart beat wildly. Each hero longed to be his chieftain's choice. Each hoped to match *his* skill against the cunning of the ogress.

In silence Finn appraised the men before him. Here stood the flower of the nation, the bravest of all Erin. Most of the men were bearded veterans of perilous adventure. Only Regan, the youngest, was yet untried. Finn never had sent him on a mission alone.

Finn studied the red-haired youth. "Fleet-footed Regan," his companions called him, for in any race he could outstrip his elders. The old warrior gazed into the youth's clear blue eyes. What he saw were courage and a yearning to prove himself.

Finn beckoned the stripling to approach. "You, Regan, come here," he boomed. "Yours—*yours alone shall be the task.*"

Regan caught his breath. Too astounded by his good fortune to say a word, he stepped out from the other men. As he knelt before Finn, his Fianna brothers shook their heads.

Some murmured, "He is too young."

"Surely, the ogress will destroy him."

"Only a miracle will bring the lad back alive."

"*Silence!*" commanded Finn, raising his hand. From his bosom he drew forth a small object that gleamed as brightly as the boy's burnished curls. Finn held up a cap woven in fine golden threads. He slipped it on the youth's head. The cap fitted as if made for Regan alone.

"Yours be the luck, Fleet-footed Regan," Finn cried. "This cap is thrice charmed. Luno, the wizard of Lochlin, made it. To extinguish the Candle of Death will require youth as well as courage. Therefore, from among all these brave men, I appoint you for the mission. But to vanquish the likes of Grana, even the stoutest heart can use a bit of magic. Take the cap, lad. it will serve you in time of need."

The Fianna brothers thundered encouragement, though many

had anxious hearts. "Luck to you," they cheered. "You'll return a hero."

Regan bowed to his chieftain. He saluted his brothers. Then he ran to the door. Swiftly he sped toward the west.

The journey was filled with peril. Beasts of prey lurked in the forest. Evil spirits leered behind stones. The woods echoed with terrifying noises. Yet young Regan feared nothing. His heart was light. His feet were fleet.

"*I* was chosen," he exulted. "Finn chose *me* from all the others —to vanquish the ogress, to destroy her power."

The youth hastened over mountains and valleys. He traversed wide pastures. He paused for neither food nor drink. Just as dusk was closing over the valley, Regan reached Grana's land. Through the trees he saw the fast-flowing Shannon. High above it, on a steep cliff, rose a gigantic rock.

"So *that* is where Grana lives," cried Regan. "That's where she burns the Candle of Death. And that," he added soberly, "is where I must surprise her this very night."

As the youth thought of scaling the slippery wall of rock, his knees trembled in spite of himself. What would happen to him if he should fall . . . if Grana spied him or heard him scraping against the side of the cliff? Whatever befell, he would be prudent, Regan resolved, impatient though he was to get on with his task. In any case, he'd have to wait until nightfall.

The young man tightened his belt. He adjusted the cap on his head. The instant his fingers touched the fine fabric, new courage surged into his heart. With caution Regan crept toward the rock. "The old hag mustn't guess I'm around," he told himself, curbing his impulse to run. At last he settled down to wait in a recess below the rock.

Gradually dusk flowed into twilight, twilight into darkness. It wasn't until the first star appeared in the sky that Regan heard a scuffling and rumbling overhead. *It's Grana*, he thought, choking back his excitement. She's lighting her candle. Soon I can climb.

As the youth sprang to his feet, he felt an irresistible urge to glance up, but just at that moment the magic cap fell over his eyes. So *that's* what it's for, Regan thought in relief. If I'd seen even the faintest glimmer of candlelight just now, Grana would soon be picking my bones!

Regan groped along the cliff. Then, his eyes still covered by the magic cap, he began his perilous ascent. Softly as a cat, scarcely daring to breathe, he pulled himself slowly from ledge to ledge. In some places the rock was so sheer that for each foot he gained, he slipped back three.

When he felt he'd been climbing for hours, Regan jumped as he heard Grana breathing—only a few yards from where he clung to the cliff. He paused to listen. The ogress is crouched on the other side of the rock, the lad concluded. The candle is somewhere near this edge. I must manage, somehow, to extinguish the flame before she gets at me.

Regan inched along. Noiselessly he pulled himself up to the rock. He could not see it. But he felt the warmth of the burning candle on his face. Before Grana saw him he sprang toward the candle, groping until his fingers closed on it. Regan snuffed out the wick swiftly. Then, snatching up the candle, he hurled it from him with a powerful thrust. The evil thing flew over the edge of the rock, landing with a hiss in the River Shannon. The waters boiled in fury. They raged and foamed, then sucked the candle down, down to the river bed.

At the same instant, the cap lifted from the lad's eyes. It did so in time for him to see Grana shoot out her hand. Now all is lost, Regan thought, as the monster fingers hovered above his head. *It was then that he jumped.* Aided by the magic of the cap, he leaped through the air at the speed of the wind. Far behind, he heard Grana bellow with rage.

"I'll eat your flesh. I'll gnaw you to bits. I'll dash your bones after my candle."

"Just try it," shouted Regan, who by now had landed safely on a rock two miles west of Grana's lair.

The lad's escape so enraged the ogress that she tried to wrench off a chunk of rock to hurl after him. She clutched the stone with her giant fingers. Then she pulled. She strained and tugged with all her might. She dragged at the rock until her face turned purple, then black as a thundercloud. Her great chest heaved like a bellow. With a tremendous twist, Grana finally loosened a huge piece of stone. Slowly she straightened her body. Then, summoning all her strength, she pitched the rock at Regan's head.

In spite of her size and the might of her arm, Grana's effort was puny compared to Regan's miraculous leap. The stone crashed down somewhere on the coast of Ireland—less than half the distance to where Regan stood. You can see the rock yet, if you search long enough. You'll know it when you find it. For plainly as the nose on your face, you'll see the gouging Grana's fingers left on the hard stone.

When the ogress realized she hadn't killed Regan, her mortification knew no end. She stamped her feet until her rock trembled. She roared with rage. At last, blind with fury, she stepped too near the edge of the cliff. With a wild shriek, she toppled into the ravine. No one ever saw Grana again. No one even searched for her body.

Great was the rejoicing in the Shannon valley. The people hailed Regan as their savior. Their gratitude knew no bounds.

When the youth returned to Finn, the chieftain welcomed him as a hero. Now Regan took his place as a proven warrior among the Fianna brotherhood. His memory never died in Erin. Bards have recited his exploits for hundreds of years. They have sung of the lad with a magic cap, who first snuffed out the Candle of Death and destroyed the ogress, then served his land with yet mightier deeds, to the end of his long, long life.

6

THE COW WHO NEVER WENT DRY

(England)

Although most monsters are evil, this is the story of one who was good. The Great Dun Cow was a monster only in size. She appeared by magic on the fells of England, and there she remained till her work was done.

For hundreds and hundreds of years folk of the fells have revered this wonderful beast. They have repeated her legend again and again, so none should forget her kindness.

The tale of the Great Dun Cow began long ago, when northwest England suffered grievous drought. Famine and misery followed its wake. Day after day the sun blazed down on the fells. The scorching rays withered the corn on the stalk. They seared the flowers in woodlands and fields. Streams and springs that never had failed now shrank to a trickle. Even the River Ribble shriveled in its bed.

While the sun stared down on the earth not a drop of rain, a shred of mist, even a small wisp of fog relieved the thirsty land. Each evening the farmers scanned the sky, praying for rain.

" 'Red at night, sailors' delight,' " they sighed. "Tomorrow will be another fair day. Unless rain falls soon, all the crops will fail."

"But what of our little ones?" mothers asked. "Already our cows have gone dry. Their calves have died, and bats fly over the fells by day."

"Another sign of no rain!" menfolk muttered, turning aside to hide their tears.

The weary days dragged on, one after another. Still the yellow sun glared down on the stubble until even crickets couldn't sing. The fells looked like a graveyard for the bones of sheep. The earth yawned with ugly cracks. After harvest failed, famine threatened the villages.

One night, after the children had gone to bed, young Robbie

59

Bowland heard his father say, "I can see no hope. We face starvation."

"Yes." Robbie's mother choked on a sob. "There's nothing left in the larder, except three shriveled turnips and a strip of salt pork."

The boy heard his mother weeping as he lay wide-eyed in the dark. He was drifting into uneasy sleep, when he thought of a plan that might help.

Before dawn, Robbie rose softly and crept down the stairs. He stared into the bucket in the corner of the kitchen. Not enough water to make a cup of tea! Robbie ran to the well, peering inside. Then his heart sank to his very boots. *The well was dry.*

Things were worse than he had supposed, Robbie admitted, scratching his sandy hair. He would have to climb to the top of the fells called Parlick, just as he'd decided last night. Water never failed up there! When he was a small boy on his grandfather's knee, the old man had told him about the Devil's Watering Pot.

"It's on the summit of Parlick," Grandfather had said, pointing to the distant hill. "The Devil himself drinks there. Now mind you, Robbie lad, nobody's *seen* him. But so long as 'Owd Nick' roams these fells, his hole will never go dry."

Robbie snatched up a pail and headed toward Parlick. He'd get a good start before the sun rose. He shivered a little at the thought of Owd Nick, wondering what he'd do if he met the Devil at his hole —then— "Nonsense," cried Robbie. He pulled himself together. "I won't let *that* scare me! I've got to find water. If I don't, everyone in the village will die."

Robbie trudged toward the hill, but the longer he walked the farther off it seemed. His knees trembled from weakness. His lips cracked with thirst. When the sun rose and beat on his head, each step was torture, each breath pain.

"Merciful Heaven," Robbie panted. "Help me get there. Let me find water before it's too late."

At last the boy sank down to rest. Whether he lay on the ground a few minutes or a few hours, Robbie couldn't say, when he told the story later. All he could remember was, that after a while he heard a sound. He thought he was dreaming. Then he heard it again. It was a *moo-mooing*, far away at first, then close at hand.

MOO-MOO-OOO-O! The sound was loud and insistent. It was next to Robbie's ear. At the same instant he heard suckings and chewings as if a hundred cows were rolling their cuds. This was no dream! Robbie rubbed his eyes. He leaped to his feet. Then he stood there gaping.

What Robbie saw couldn't be! Towering above him was a gigantic dun-colored cow. She was high as a fortress, wide as a moat. It was *she* who was making the noises he'd heard. The monster was chewing her cud!

Robbie was too astonished to utter a word. The Great Dun Cow stared at him from immense brown eyes. She tossed her head in friendly fashion. Then she mooed again.

Robbie was so small beside the cow that he had to crane his neck to see her face. Her expression was so kind, her eyes so gentle, that the lad felt no fear.

"Who are you?" Robbie asked. "Where did you come from? What do you want?"

"MOO-OO-O," said the cow, advancing a step.

For the first time Robbie noticed that the monster was heavy with milk. "Why, you're a *magic* cow," he shouted joyfully. "You want to be milked! You've come to bring us food and drink."

Robbie gazed up at the Great Dun Cow. She gazed down at him. Then, as he told his mother afterward, she nodded her head!

Robbie set his pail under the creature. But when he looked up, he realized he never could reach her udder.

"What shall I do?" wailed the boy. "I'd have to have arms two yards long to milk you—and only a giant would have the strength!"

Robbie had scarcely spoken when the milk started to flow of its own accord. The liquid streamed into the bucket without spilling a drop. The youth stood back and watched with wonder. The milk was rich and yellow—richer and yellower than any he'd ever seen. He reached out a finger to taste a drop. Then he cupped both hands so the milk could trickle down his throat. Almost at once, Robbie felt strong again.

"Thank you, dear cow, *thank you,*" Robbie cried, when the pail was full as his stomach. The stream ceased as miraculously as it had begun. Tears of joy rolled down the boy's cheeks. He threw his arms around the cow's great leg. "You have saved us from starvation," he exclaimed. "You have come just in time."

The Great Dun Cow blinked her round eyes at Robbie. She

flicked a fly off with her long tail. Then she tapped the ground with an impatient hoof.

"It was plain as could be," Robbie told the villagers later. "She was saying, 'Get along home with your milk. Be quick about it, too. Tell your neighbors I'm here to feed them.' Hurry," the boy urged. "The cow has milk for everyone."

The village people were so famished that they didn't even pause to marvel at Robbie's story. They snatched up buckets and basins, teapots, jugs—anything to hold milk. Then they scrambled up the fells behind Robbie.

The people shouted with joy when they beheld the Great Dun Cow on the crest of the hill. There she stood like a mother awaiting her children. In the golden sunshine the long curved horns on her head gleamed like a crown.

As the procession approached her, the Great Dun Cow lowed, "MOO-OO-O-O."

"She's inviting you to get your milk," cried Robbie.

The hungry folk surged up the hill. To each one, in turn, the giant beast gave milk—enough to drink, to carry home. After that, she remained on the fells. From east to west, north to south, she roamed. She fed the hungry in hamlets for miles about. Everyone blessed her. "As good as the Great Dun Cow" grew to be a saying among those she fed.

"Robbie Bowland's a hero," the farmers agreed. "He set out alone to find the Devil's Watering Pot—a thing none of us dared do. Instead of water, he found the cow. The boy's courage, and *her* milk, have saved us from death."

Before long the people of the fells regained their strength, for the Great Dun Cow was generous as she was big. Little children, once wan with hunger, again had rosy cheeks. They loved the cow. Every day they romped beside her. When youngsters refused to eat their porridge, or cried at bedtime, all mothers had to say was, "If you don't behave, you can't play with the cow tomorrow," and the little ones sprouted wings!

Gradually the countryside prospered again. Finally the rains came and farmers planted new crops. After the first harvest, the folk of the fells were happy and well fed. Their gratitude to the Great

Dun Cow was boundless. They brought her new oats and a load of hay, then dancd and sang around her feet.

Now while this rejoicing was going on, a wicked witch who lived on distant Pendle Hill was muttering magic words in her cave.

"Come, drought,
Come, famine,
Come, pain and trouble,"

the witch droned as she stirred an evil-smelling brew with a long black spoon. Just as the old hag paused to add a shark's fin and a green snake's eye, a demon burst into the cavern.

"To the west, a monster cow's feeding on the fells of Longridge," panted the demon. "She's been roaming there weeks. She's lifted the drought you sent to destroy the land and starve the people. Now they're prosperous and fat—thanks to the beast's milk, and the rains she's brought."

"*What!*" screamed the witch, quivering with rage. She stamped her feet until Pendle Hill shook. She tore out tufts of gray hair. "A stupid cow dares defy *me*, dares undo the spells *I've* put on the land!"

The Witch of Pendle's fury so terrorized the demon that he fled from the cave—just in time to escape the boiling brew she threw at his heels. The old hag snatched up her peaked hat. Then she mounted her broomstick. Under one arm she tucked a milking stool tall as a house. From the other she dangled a bottomless pail. By bright moonlight she flew swiftly for Longridge.

"So a monster brute chews her cud on the fells," sneered the witch as she whistled through the air. "Just wait! I'll teach her to meddle in my affairs. A cow with magic milk—pfui! After tonight, she won't moo again!"

It was nearly dawn when the witch spied the cow browsing on top of the hill. Without a word the old crone zoomed to earth. She plopped her pail under the beast, then slammed down her milking stool. With a hideous howl, the witch flew to the seat. Then, pushing back her hat, she set to work.

The witch milked, and she milked, as the sun rose in the sky. She milked through the noonday heat. She milked when the birds dozed on their perches. As the sun sank behind the rim of the fells, the old hag was still milking.

When twilight began to creep across the fells, the Great Dun Cow turned her head. For an instant she stared at the tight-lipped witch, perched on her tall milking stool. Then the cow kicked the stool.

With a frantic scream the witch sailed through the air and crashed to the ground. She rolled over and over in the prickly heather. In less than a second the pail hurtled after her, engulfing the witch in a torrent of yellow milk.

"Help me . . . *help*," screeched the witch, beating the air with her skinny arms in an effort to swim.

"MOO-OO-O," said the cow placidly as she walked away in the twilight.

The witch struggled and screamed until the shadows deepened into darkness. At last her body dissolved in the magic milk, which sank far down into the earth. Then the spell of the Witch of Pendle was broken forever. No sign of the conflict remained.

The same night that the witch perished, the Great Dun Cow disappeared from the fells. When Robbie Bowland and the other boys and girls trooped out next day to frolic around the cow's feet, they couldn't find their friend. They hunted and called all that day, and the day after that, and for many days thereafter. Their elders joined in the search. Great was the mourning of old and young when convinced, at last, that they never should see the good cow again.

"Some bewitchment caused her end," the farmers concluded. "We might have saved her if we'd tied a lucky stone around her leg."

"Or made her a cross of whitethorn twig," said the women, wiping tears from their eyes. "That's a *sure* charm against witches."

There were others who knew—just as you and I do—that neither lucky stones nor charms could keep the Great Dun Cow from going away. She stayed with her people until they needed her no more. But she has lived in their hearts for hundreds of years since. Not even the wicked Witch of Pendle had power to destroy what was generous and good.

7

THE WICKED SQUIRE

(Channel Islands: Jersey)

Many hundreds of years ago, a noisy singing dragon lived in Jersey, loveliest of the islands that lie in the Channel, south of England and west of France. The islands, which look like bright pebbles some giant has strewn in the sea, draw both monsters and men to their shores.

The Dragon of Jersey was as wicked as any dragon that ever lived. At first no one *saw* him, for he hid away in a cave. But once he had discovered the lush Saint Lawrence valley, people *heard* him. He would sing at night, before he raided the farms. Though his voice started rumbly and low, it gradually grew in volume. It rolled out louder as he swooped through the valley on powerful black wings. His singing sounded like thunder by the time he had passed through the hills. The singing echoed along the river bed. As the dragon approached the homes of men, folk could hear these words:

> "My head is thick as iron,
> My body is strong as steel,
> My claws are hard as beaten brass.
> No man can make me feel."

Once the dragon had ceased his singing, folk knew what to expect. In the morning they'd find cattle and horses wandering in a daze. They'd see orchards stripped of apples and pears, bins emptied of grain. And if they had left ewe lambs in the fold, or baby pigs in the pen, there would be no sign of the creatures.

The dragon hummed with delight as he listened to the farmers moan, "Now that he's stolen our youngest and best, he'll soon have our cows and sheep."

"Right you are, idiots," snortled the dragon as he noisily crunched a young goat's bones. "These tender pickings won't last forever. Once *they* are gone, look out!" So speaking, the dragon would sing softly, though loud enough for frightened farmers to hear:

"My claws are hard as beaten brass."

The dragon's claws—curved and sharp as an eagle's talons, but many times bigger—could tear a wild boar or a man to tatters. The nails gleamed in the sun as the dragon hurled a bone at a vulture circling overhead. The dragon shrieked with laughter when the bird fell dead. "That will teach *you* to watch every morsel I put in my mouth!" he hissed. Then, after dusting his shiny wings and the prickly black mane that rose from his neck, he coiled his length around a hill. Then he went to sleep, to dream of his next raid.

As weeks lengthened into months, the farmers heard the dragon's song more frequently. At first they were too terrified to do anything. But the day they discovered that the dragon had flown away with Paul Morin's best milch cow, they yelled, "If we don't kill the dragon, he'll take *all* our beasts. Then we'll be ruined. We'll starve!"

That very night the farmers, armed with pitchforks and scythes, hid behind a haystack in a field. Near the haystack they placed a little horned cow. "When the dragon starts to sing, we'll be ready," they said. "We'll rush out all together when he swoops for the cow."

It was close to midnight when they heard the singing. The men gripped their weapons. Their teeth chattered with fear. But instead of zooming down into the field, the dragon bellowed until dishes fell from racks in the farms. He shook the entire parish by lashing the hill with his tail. He never did come for the little horned cow.

Next morning when the farmers went to the fields, they found the wheat trampled, potatoes and onions strewn on the ground. They wept at the destruction. "First our animals, now our crops," they cried. "The dragon won't rest till he eats *us.*"

"That he won't do," shouted the youths, shaking their fists. "We must get help. Pitchforks and scythes are nothing against wings and hard claws. Let us beg the valiant young Seigneur of Hambaie, Renaud the Knight, to destroy the dragon. That young man slew the two-headed monster of Provence single-handed, people say. Only skill and arms such as his can kill *this* foe."

67

"The great seigneur . . . help us!" gasped the elders, scandalized. "Alas, youth is impertinent. Why should the knight help poor farmers? Who would even dare *ask* him?"

"Let me try," Anton, the oldest lad, cried. "I'll go to Normandy in my fishing boat. The knight is young—scarcely older than I. Folk say he's kind and good. I'm not afraid to ask his help—even if he *does* have a title, riches, lands."

"Let Anton go," the other youths urged, pressing around their elders. "If he fails, we can't be worse off than now. Renaud never was one to stand by and do nothing when others need help."

"The seigneur's father was this island's friend," put in a young boy. "His son won't fail us."

"And if he did slay the dragon," another lad said, "we could give him a tenth of our island yield."

The older men hemmed and hawed. They pulled at their beards, and cleared their throats. But, in the end, they agreed that the youths might be right. They allowed Anton to go to Normandy. "He can plead our cause best," they said. "He's not afraid."

When Anton had beached his boat on the shore of France, he hurried to the seigneur's castle. Though the stately battlements and towers awed the youth, he boldly knocked at the gate. "I must see the knight at once," he told the surly squire who peered through the wrought-iron grill.

"And who are *you?*" sneered the squire, eying the stranger's patched jacket, his tousled hair. "What's your business with my master, may I ask?"

"That I can tell him only," said Anton. "It is a matter of life and death. Hurry, man," he, urged, for the squire only scowled. He made no move to unlock the gate. "I come from Jersey. We must get help."

"And what you'll get are the dogs—if you don't clear out," yelled the servant insolently. "Return to your island. The master isn't home. And if he were, he wouldn't waste time on a ragged lout like you!"

"I'll not leave until the seigneur hears my story," cried Anton, winking back tears of rage. "Can't you understand—I *must* see him?"

Just when the youth realized he was wasting his breath, a voice called from within. "Blaise, Blaise, what is the matter? Whom do I hear at the gate?"

"Only a beggar," growled the squire, with a menacing glance at Anton. "I've sent him away."

"Then go after him at once," commanded the voice sternly. "How often have I told you never to send a beggar away?"

All the while the squire was turning the key in the lock, he muttered terrifying threats to Anton. "I'll be listening at the keyhole," he warned, "so don't think you can give me away."

But when Blaise had led the stranger to the knight, the servant knelt at his feet. "Forgive me, Master," said the squire humbly. "I didn't think you'd want to see this man." Then he slipped from the room.

The young knight greeted Anton with a smile. He seated him in a chair. Then Renaud listened gravely to the story of the marauding dragon. "You, Seigneur, are our only hope," the lad ended. "Things have gone from bad to worse. Soon we'll be without animals or crops. Who knows what will happen then?"

The seigneur's handsome face darkened as he learned of the dragon's ravages. He banged the table with his clenched fist. "I'll slay the monster," he cried. "I can't rest as long as my neighbors suffer this scourge. My father would not endure such an outrage without offering help. Neither shall his son."

The squire, listening at the keyhole, shook with fury when Renaud said, "Go home, lad. Tell your people I am coming to do battle with the dragon. Blaise will prepare my arms at once. We'll land in the east at Grouville Bay. No one is to greet us. We must take the dragon by surprise."

"So," Blaise muttered viciously. "Brave Renaud is going to risk *my* neck, as well as his own, on this stupid venture. What an idiot I've been, to think he'd settle down, once he won the Lady Genevieve as his bride!"

At thought of the lovely maiden—with the thick gold plaits against her white brow, the eyes like blue violets, the rosebud mouth —his eyes burned with envy. "She should be mine," he whispered, clenching his fists until the nails dug into the flesh. "*Mine*, not his, I say. Without *my* help Renaud could not have rescued her from the tower where ruffians held her captive. *I* held the ladder when he carried her down. *I* gave the signal when all was clear."

Blaise broke off suddenly. An evil thought crawled through his mind. "There may be a way," he mumbled, a treacherous smile twisting his lips. "Why should I be a servant to the end of my days? I'd be as handsome as my master if *I* had silken hose, velvet doublet, and a jewel on my hand! Why shouldn't *I* have glory, fame?"

As Blaise plotted against his master, he forgot how Renaud had freed him when he languished in a dungeon, how the knight had nursed him through fever, and then—when Blaise was without money, friends —brought him to the castle as his trusted squire.

While the wicked servant schemed behind the door, Renaud was bidding his guest farewell.

"You are so good, Seigneur, so kind," cried Anton, his eyes shining with gratitude. "May heaven guide your mission of mercy. But I beg you, dear Seigneur, take care," he whispered, remembering the squire's treacherous eyes. "The dragon may not be the *only* peril you face."

Though the lad's words puzzled the knight, he forgot them when his servant approached with respectful smiles. Blaise listened attentively to Renaud's plan to help his neighbors. "We must deliver them from the dragon at once," the knight concluded. "His ravages grow more terrifying each passing night. Prepare our boat without delay. Have my suit of armor ready, my best sword."

Blaise watched with jealous eyes as the young knight hurried to the garden to join his bride. "As usual, he leaves me with all the work, while *he* walks with his lady," grumbled the squire, letting Renaud's sword clatter to the floor. As he set to polishing the shining blade, he kept mumbling, "Just wait—*my* turn will come to play the great nobleman!"

The sun was shining brightly next day when the seigneur and his servant landed at Grouville Bay. The air was warm and soft. As Blaise helped Renaud into his chain mail, the knight scanned the hills to the west. "Somewhere yonder the dragon hides in his lair," he said. "We must be cautious. I'll lead the way. You follow, alert to danger from the rear."

"Have no fear, Master. You can trust me," said Blaise, testing the edge of his dagger between forefinger and thumb.

As Renaud advanced toward the hills, he moved with easy grace. Blaise followed behind, his heart consumed by envy. How I hate him, the servant brooded. He always leads. I follow. I guard him from the rear. I carry his weapons, like a drudging beast. *He* wins fame, riches, love. *I* am only a squire!

Envy tormented Blaise until he forgot where he was. He jumped when Renaud whispered, *"Stop!"* Glancing up, Blaise saw his master standing motionless, one finger pressed to his lips. From the distance came a low rumble. At first it sounded like waves against the rocks off-shore. Then the rumble roared into words. They thundered across the meadows.

> "My head is thick as iron,
> My body is strong as steel,
> My claws are hard as beaten brass.
> No man can make me feel!"

"It's the dragon!" Renaud exclaimed. He paused, lost in thought. Then turning to his squire, he said slowly, "If I interpret the song rightly, there is no use in trying to pierce his body or bash in his head. The only way to kill the dragon is by way of his throat! I'll take my sword, Blaise. Stand by with your dagger."

Renaud had scarcely spoken when the ground began to quake. Fearful growls followed, then hideous howls. Renaud sprang forward. Blaise jumped behind a tree. A mass of fog billowed over the hill. From surging puffs of smoke and mist peered the head of the dragon.

The knight saw the jagged teeth inside the gaping jaws. He saw the long red tongue forked at the tip, the round bulging eyes that could see on all sides at once. Renaud barely had time to leap before the monster swooped toward him, claws outstretched.

Once he'd started, the dragon—who was big as a house—couldn't stop. Missing Renaud by an inch, he crashed on down the hill. At the bottom he landed in a writhing mass of wings, tail and snapping jaws.

Renaud roared with laughter as the dragon snorted and struggled in mortification and rage. "Pick yourself up," he jeered from the hill. "Try again—if you dare!" The knight brandished his sword so the steel edge glinted in the sun.

71

"No man can make me feel," bellowed the dragon so loudly that peasants plowing the fields in Normandy heard the noise.

"Come on, then," Renaud yelled. "*I'll* make you feel!"

The dragon charged at him. But Renaud stood ready for the monster. As he lunged at the knight, Renaud grasped his sword in both hands. He rammed it down the dragon's open jaws until it pierced the yawning throat.

Blood gushed over the hillside and the dying dragon screamed at his foe. Renaud lightly dodged the thrashing of the long steely tail. He kept far from the clutches of the hard claws.

When the dragon had breathed his last, Renaud glanced about for Blaise. "Where are you?" he called sharply. "Come here quickly. Help with my armor. The dragon is dead. The island folk are safe."

"I'm coming, Master," Blaise called, scrambling from behind the tree. "I was fetching water to bathe your face and refresh you. I was close behind you while you fought. Only *you* had cunning to slay this dragon. The islanders will bless you to the end of time."

As he ran toward his master, Blaise fingered the dagger at his belt. Now is the time to kill him, the squire thought. If I do—if I get away before anyone comes—I'll say the dragon killed *him*. I'll say *I* slew the monster, to avenge my master's death!

Dreams of fame . . . of wealth . . . of tricking Renaud's wife into wedding *him,* dazzled the wicked squire's mind as he knelt beside the knight. Blaise removed Renaud's armor. The servant murmured words of praise, of pride in the seigneur's valorous deed, as he chafed his master's wrists. Then, without warning, Blaise whipped out his dagger. He sank the blade deep into Renaud's neck.

Horror and disbelief shone in the eyes of the dying man. "You . . . Blaise . . . my trusted friend," he gasped staring into his squire's face. "It was of *you* Anton tried to warn me! May heaven help your soul."

Blaise buried his master near the dead dragon. The squire marked the grave with a wooden cross. "In case anyone questions the story of the devoted servant," he cried. Then he hurried back to the boat.

As Blaise approached the coast of Normandy, he saw the Lady Genevieve pacing the beach. She kept glancing toward the boat, her hand shading her eyes against the sun. Blaise's heart beat wildly as he studied the slender figure in white, the hair like burnished gold, the

flower face. "If I'm clever, you'll soon be mine," the servant muttered. "I'll rule yonder castle as the new seigneur."

His dark eyes glittered with greed as he moored the boat. Genevieve rushed toward the squire, wringing her hands. "Where is he?" she cried, scanning the empty boat. "Where is my lord? Why do you return alone?"

"I bring bitter news." Blaise choked as he knelt before his mistress. "The dragon has slain your husband—my dearest friend and master—the valiant seigneur," he stammered.

Genevieve swayed at the terrible words. When she could speak, she implored, "Tell me everything—to the least detail."

Then Blaise described the conflict which he, Blaise, had shared with his master. "He fought like a tiger," the squire said. "After a long and bloody battle, we forced the dragon back, an inch at a time. Then, when the seigneur lifted his sword to inflict the death blow, the dragon lashed at the knight with his tail. It was then I snatched the sword from my master's hand. I sank the steel point into the dragon's throat when he opened his jaws to roar."

"And the seigneur?" cried the bereaved wife through her tears.

"He died in my arms," said Blaise sadly. "Would *I* had died, instead! His last thoughts were of you. 'Tell the Lady Genevieve of my love,' he gasped. 'For my sake, take care of her, Blaise. Tell her—'" The squire broke off suddenly, as if too modest, too overcome by grief to continue.

"'Tell her'—*what*?" Genevieve insisted. "Hold nothing back."

With apparent effort Blaise pulled himself together. Then he spoke slowly. "'Tell her,' he said, 'my wish is that she wed you, faithful friend, in reward for your courage. To avenge my death you slew the dragon, at peril to your own life.' Clearly, my master was out of his head," the squire added, observing the astonishment on the lady's face. "These last words were the ravings of a dying man."

In the days and weeks that followed, the Lady Genevieve pondered what she supposed was her husband's final wish. Though terror of discovery tormented Blaise night and day, he never pressed the young widow. But when she said one day, "I can no longer disregard Renaud's dying words. Out of love for him, I'll marry you," the squire's relief knew no bounds. The dream he had killed for was reality, at last! Once he became seigneur, he had nothing more to fear.

Yet after the wedding, the squire soon discovered it wasn't easy to follow in the footsteps of the knight. Though Blaise showered his wife with silks and jewels, though he stroked her golden hair, he shrank from the trust in her violet eyes. He now dressed in velvets. He wore the ring with his master's arms, yet Blaise knew the servants despised him. "Evil days are upon us," they whispered. "God pity our sweet mistress."

As autumn crept into winter, and chill winds whistled up from the sea, Blaise couldn't help remembering his dying master's eyes. He thought of the lonely grave on the hill. Then the former squire wandered from room to room in the castle. He sat by the fire, in Renaud's empty chair. "They are all talking behind my back," the new seigneur said, "but no one can guess the truth."

But once Blaise began thinking of that last look of astonished horror in Renaud's eyes, terrifying dreams plagued him at night. At first he only tossed and turned on his pillow. Then he talked in his sleep. Once Blaise moaned, "Now is the time!" Then he shouted wildly, "No, no—it's the *dragon's* blood on my sleeve!"

Night after night, Genevieve wakened the tortured man, out of pity. He suffers from shock, she thought, from slaying the dragon, from grief when his beloved master died. And yet—Genevieve noticed that her husband shook with terror when she roused him. Sweat beaded his forehead. When she tried to soothe him to sleep, he always demanded, "Tell me, did I talk in my sleep? What did I say?" After such questions, Blaise refused to close his eyes the rest of the night.

Nightmares continued to trouble Blaise. He grew listless and pale—afraid, Genevieve thought, to go to sleep. It was only then that she suspected some evil deed preyed on his mind. So, instead of rousing Blaise from sleep when he talked, his wife decided she'd listen to every word.

At last a night came when Blaise sobbed and moaned, "Oh, wretched me! Shall I never find peace? Must I always be miserable because of murdering my master?"

Without waiting to hear more, Genevieve wrapped herself in her cloak. Shaking with horror, and with new grief, she crept from the castle. Then she ran to the church. She roused the priest from his prayers. "Come quickly," she implored. "My husband is confessing a terrible crime in his sleep."

75

The priest hurried back to the castle with the lady. When he had listened to Blaise's guilty secret, the holy man wakened him. Then he summoned the guards to haul the wicked squire off to prison. For many days he languished in a dungeon. Later Blaise was condemned to die for slaying his master.

Genevieve, the Lady of Hambaie, now mourned Renaud's death more deeply than before. She decided to devote her life to good works. "I shall enter a convent," she said. "But first, I must visit the spot where my husband slew the dragon. I'll build a chapel there, in memory of my brave knight."

Though almost nine centuries have passed since Renaud killed the noisy singing dragon, people of Jersey still point to a circular mound west of Grouville Bay. On top of the hill, built of limpet shells and stones, mixed with rubble and earth, two chapels stand under one roof.

"That's the *Hougue Bie,* the Mound of Hambaie," islanders tell you. "His lady raised it over the seigneur's bones. The older chapel is the one *she* built. Jerusalem Chapel is the other one. That was erected years and years later."

From her convent in Normandy, they go on to say, the Lady gazed at the Hougue Bie every day, and prayed for the soul of her murdered lord.

8

THE NANNY GOAT'S CORNER
(Channel Islands: Guernsey)

Off the rugged south coast of Guernsey is a sheltered cove called Saints' Bay. Now, as for hundreds of years, restless waves pound the jagged rocks of the shore. Driftweed, or *vraic,* clothes the rocks with a dark shaggy growth that island farmers hoard like gold.

Twice each year, starting with the first spring tide after Candlemas, and again in midsummer, farmers go to the bays with short sickles to cut the harvest of vraic. "Plowed into the fields, it makes the grain grow," they tell you "Burned on the hearth, it keeps the cottage snug."

To cut armfuls of wet driftweed and pile it high on a cart drawn up to the shore is hard heavy work even today. "But in olden times, it wasn't the *work* people dreaded," the folk about Saints' Bay explain. "It was *la Biche!* Vraikers never knew *what* might happen, if she reared from her corner after dark. She might tip the cart over, or scatter dripping vraic over the lane. She might bewitch the farmers' beasts—even the farmer himself! One couldn't tell about la Biche!"

La Biche, a huge, gray nanny goat, was a very old monster in Guernsey. Sometimes homecoming vraikers saw her. Sometimes they didn't. But sensible men knew she was *there,* waiting to pounce on their carts.

Le Coin de la Biche, the Nanny Goat's Corner, was a triangular piece of ground, off Saints' Bay Road, on the way to La Villette. In olden times the place, which lay between two fields, bristled with brambles, tall grasses and weeds. No farmer dared touch it with sickle or scythe, for fear of the Goat. She brought bad luck to all who roused her wrath.

To this day you can see the haunted spot, though time has changed the neighborhood. And you'll hear a story that still chills the blood.

The tale is about Gustave and Pierre, a farmer and his hired lad, and the night they turned their two-wheeled cart into the winding, pebbly road that led inland from the sea. The cart was piled high with wet dripping vraic. The driftweed glistened bright yellow, orange and brown in the late sun. The axles of Gustave's wagon clacked and groaned under the burden—heavy even for the three oxen and two horses which tugged and strained at the reins. The going was painful and slow for the beasts, in spite of Gustave's encouraging words.

"Steady there, old chap," he cried, tightening his hold on the reins as the lead ox stumbled on a bump. In those days, the road was only a channel bordered by hawthorn and gorse. Water from swollen inland rivers rushed to the sea at the animals' feet. The lane was dim and gloomy, though the sun hadn't set. Pierre was jumpy. He kept glancing this way and that. He clutched at the sides of the cart, as it bumpity-bumped over rocks and sand ridges.

"What's the matter, lad?" Gustave asked kindly, easing the animals over a bad spot. "In another hour this rough bit will be behind us. We'll have smoother going, once we reach yonder fields."

The *fields*—the word set Pierre's teeth chattering in an agony of terror. Shivers crept up his spine. Yet it wasn't the fields, *but what lay between them,* that made his voice quaver.

"B-bu-but what if we meet the N-Na-Nanny Goat?" he blurted. "What then? We've g-got to pass her Corner—and it's nearly dark!"

"So *that's* what is bothering you!" cried Gustave. He guffawed so loudly the animals jumped. "Surely you don't believe those silly stories about the haunted Corner, the mad power of la Biche! Why, I've jogged up and down this crooked lane for twenty-odd years. *I've* never met the Goat."

"But if we should?" Pierre persisted, trying to keep his voice steady. "When I was small, Grandfather told such scary things about her."

"Bah," Gustave cried, flicking his reins. "Those were stories to amuse a wee chap. Besides, if we should meet the Goat, what could she do to us? We're only poor vraikers, going home with our load. We've nothing the old Nanny wants."

As the road turned rougher, Gustave fell silent. To guide the beasts through the bumpy channel took all his skill. As the cart screeched along with no sign of trouble, the lad breathed easier. Of course, Gustave was right. Still, Pierre couldn't help remembering what his grandfather had told him as a child.

"Never go near the Nanny Goat's Corner," the old man had warned. "One never knows what she'll do! Why, my grandfather's father told *him*—and he told me—what la Biche did when folks first decided to build Saint Martin's Church."

Pierre thought of the harrowing story now. Hundreds of years ago, when the islanders chose the Corner as the site for their sanctuary, nobody knew the land belonged to the Goat. *That* they didn't discover until they'd fetched granite blocks from the quarries, oak logs from the forest, and masons and stonecutters from Normandy.

"Do you know, lad, what happened once they'd broken ground, once they'd started to build the church?" the old man asked Pierre. "One night, *everything vanished*—granite, logs, mortar, tools! In the morning there wasn't a trace of them left. Even the hole in the ground was no longer there. Green grass was growing on top."

Pierre shivered now, just as he had long ago when his grandfather said, "The entire parish was in terrible turmoil. For it was plain as plain could be, some witch or devil haunted the place! Yet, folk said, stone and wood don't *vanish*—even with demons about. Then they searched the ground. Finally a young boy discovered the things that were lost. He found them laid in neat piles in the parish of La Beilleuse!

"The builders were stubborn," the old man continued, shaking his white head. "More than once they attempted to build on the place they'd picked out. But every time they brought the materials over, unseen hands moved tools and all back to La Beilleuse in the night. At last the people—now thoroughly frightened—cried, 'It's a sign! Bad luck will haunt us forever, if we don't heed it.'"

Things didn't go well, Pierre's grandfather had said, until parishioners built the church at La Beilleuse—where it still stands. Yet try as they might, people couldn't discover the awful power that had thwarted their plans. Pierre's spine prickled at the rest of the tale—when the priest learned the truth.

"It was on a night in autumn, when he couldn't sleep," the boy's grandfather said. "The priest was restless. He went to his window. He peered down at the gravestones in the churchyard below. They shone pale white in the moonlight. Huge owls huddled black in the branches of the spreading yews. Bats flitted noiselessly from tree to tree. As the priest stared at the eerie scene, he drew back in terror. For there, under his window, he saw a huge gray creature. She was dancing in and out among the graves!

"And then," Pierre's grandfather whispered in his ear, "as the

priest watched, *the creature vanished*! After that the poor man didn't live long, people say. He never told a soul what he'd seen—not until the night he died. 'It was the Goat!' he gasped with his last breath. 'It was on *her* Corner we tried to build the church. Warn my people . . . never to go there.' "

Pierre was so lost in the story that he jumped when Gustave spoke.

"We've passed the worst now," he said cheerfully. "With the animals pulling as they are now, we'll reach La Villette before long. And then, lad, we'll go to the vraikers' harvest party. We'll soon be passing the fields."

The *fields,* thought Pierre wildly. Yes—if we get by the Corner. That lies between them. By stretching his neck, the youth could glimpse it now. He tried to hide his fear but his hands shook.

"Still dreading the Goat?" chuckled Gustave, watching Pierre with amusement. "Before you know it, you'll be dancing with pretty girls at the party. You'll be stuffing yourself with raisin buns."

But Gustave had barely spoken when Pierre saw something that made him shake from head to foot. Slowly, from the bramble patch close to the lane, a dreadful head rose. In the deepening twilight the youth could see that the head belonged to a furry gray body. Then he distinguished two curving horns—and worse than that, two yellow eyes. They turned and stared at him, not blinking once. Like balls of fire, they gleamed through the dusk.

Only when the gray body reared from the briars did Pierre yell, "It's the Nanny Goat!"

From that moment the lad couldn't remember what happened next, except that the beasts shied. Gustave grabbed his whip. He lashed it through the air as he stood up in his cart. The horses and oxen strained and pulled with all their might. Yet in spite of their valiant efforts, the wagon wheels didn't budge an inch.

Too terrified to move until then, Pierre glanced behind. When he found himself gazing into the Goat's monstrous eyes, he shrieked, "She's got us, Gustave. We're lost!"

Gustave turned his head. There was the Nanny Goat on her hind legs. She stood there motionless, staring from baleful yellow eyes. Her powerful forepaws rested on the vraic. She was holding the cart down so four-and-twenty oxen couldn't move it.

Though dazed with fright, Pierre obeyed Gustave's sharp order to get out of the cart. "Quick, lad," he cried, jumping to the ground, "before she rolls us downhill, or tramples us to death. Unharness the horses. I'll take the oxen. We'll get them to the village. We'll leave the cart behind. Hurry!"

It was almost dawn before the men got the beasts home. Pierre tumbled into bed, too frightened to sleep. When he dozed off, at last, he kept seeing the pale yellow eyes of la Biche, her great curving horns. When Gustave shook his shoulder, the lad screamed.

"Don't be afraid," the older man said. "It's time to get up. After we've drunk some tea, we must go back to the lane for our, cart."

Pierre, now wide awake, shouted, *"what*—after last night?"

"That we must," said Gustave, handing the lad a cup of strong tea. *"Go back we must* if we want to eat. We have a fine harvest of vraic, to keep us the winter. The cart we need on the farm."

"But the animals—" objected Pierre, upsetting his cup. Two oxen and one horse had gone lame just before they reached home in the morning.

"We've still got one good ox and a horse," said Gustave, striding toward the barn.

"But—but—the Nanny Goat," Pierre stammered. "What about *her?* She'll bewitch us, or gore us with her horns."

"She'll be gone—now she's taught us a lesson," said Gustave, with a confidence he didn't feel.

When the youth saw that nothing he could say would change Gustave's mind, he helped him drive the animals down the road. Pierre was too shaken by now to say anything. But as they approached the Goat's Corner, there was no sign of the monster. There was no imprint of the body in the grass. No hoofmarks showed in the mud. He might have thought their adventure was nightmare—but there stood the cart in the middle of the lane. Their precious driftweed was unharmed. When they hitched the horse and the ox to the wagon, they pulled it home with ease.

"I was wrong, Pierre," Gustave admitted as they rumbled toward the village. "I thought the Goat wasn't real! Now I know she is. She'll always haunt her Corner for folks who claim she isn't there. But if they believe she *is,* she won't harm them."

Once Gustave had come to this conclusion, he never saw the Goat again. You can still see where her Corner was—but whether *you* see la Biche or not, depends upon you!

9

JACK AND THE THREE DEMONS

(Ireland)

Once on a time a churlish young fellow named Jack lived on a run-down farm, this side of Killarney. Nothing ever prospered on the place. The starved soil yielded a sorry living to the farmer and his wife, Ellen. The potatoes died from blight. The corn shriveled on the stalk in early frost.

Jack was so mean that the neighbors couldn't abide him. He always imagined people were taking things from him—though he didn't have anything worth stealing. There was his elbow chair, for example. Everyone who set foot in the house sat in *that*—though Jack had made it with his own hands, to rest his own bones in. As for his wooden wall box where he kept tools for mending his brogues, neighbors were always asking for a length of thread and a needle, a bit of wax, or the awl to patch together *their* shoes. As if these things weren't enough to try a body's patience, there was the sycamore outside the door. Every stranger who passed wanted a walking stick from that tree!

Jack was so disagreeable to everyone that when his cow wouldn't give milk and his horse went lame, the couple found themselves in dire need—with no one to help them. The neighbors never offered a pat of butter from their churning, a measure of meal, or even a mutton bone for soup because of Jack's uncivil tongue.

As things went from bad to worse, Ellen felt lucky when she managed a meal of thin gruel and soda bread. Though she knew that her husband's rude ways caused much of their suffering, she didn't say a word. Jack, who sneered at everyone else, never did a good turn in his life. If a lost stranger stopped at the door or a beggar asked for a copper, Jack didn't even offer a crust. *He'd* never asked help from any man. They'd better expect none from him!

One day when Ellen watched Jack saddling the skinny mare, he said curtly, "I'm going to Witty Fair today. I won't be home until late."

83

From the door Ellen saw the horse jog over the moor with his master. What right did he have, going to a fair? He'd spend the few shillings they had received from the hay. There wasn't enough in the larder to feed a bird! Wiping her eyes on her apron, Ellen went back to her scrubbing.

It was close to midnight when Jack, still befuddled by ale, started home by way of Dead Man's Gully. He was surprised to find himself near the river. Why had he taken *this* way home—in the dark of night? Dreadful things had happened here. They'd found Ned O'Toole's body on this path, a bloody knife in his back. People whispered of other murders, too. Tom Flaherty had met death here, though they'd never caught the robbers who had done him in. Ghosts and goblins haunted the gully—everyone knew that. Yet here he was, Jack thought, riding through the horrid place alone at night.

By now Jack was so frightened he decided he'd pray. But he hadn't prayed for so long he had forgotten how, so he bargained.

"Merciful Heaven, get me out of here alive," cried Jack, shaking from head to foot. "If you do, I promise to be a better man. I'll help beggars and strangers. I'll give them shelter and food. I won't get drunk or be mean to Ellen. I'll—I'll—"

Jack's teeth chattered until he couldn't go on. He almost fainted when he heard a low moan. Gooseflesh prickled all over his body. Sweat covered his forehead.

"Wh-who's there?" cried Jack, thinking of ghosts.

"A stranger, lost in the dark." The reply came feebly. "Help me. In Heaven's name, help me. I tried to cross the river . . . but I'll die . . . unless . . ."

The voice trailed off. Jack leaped from his horse, though he wanted to run. It's a test, he thought, to see if I meant what I said. In the darkness Jack fumbled through the long grasses. He felt along the damp ground until his fingers touched the cold body of an old man. Jack lifted the stranger to the saddle. The young farmer wrapped the old man in his coat. Then Jack jumped up behind the man. He held his arms about him, clucking to the mare.

The horse needed no urging to leave the dark gully. She shot across the stony path until she reached the open moor. Then the animal headed for home, as if unaware of the double burden on her

84

back. Still marveling at his lucky escape, Jack glanced down at the motionless form.

"Nothing's too good for you, old man," Jack said. "You saved my life tonight. I'll try to save yours."

The stranger was still unconscious when Jack carried him into the cabin. In the candlelight Jack saw that he was half-starved, incredibly old. His white beard swept his hollow chest.

"Quick, Ellen," Jack called, rousing his wife. "We'll put the old man in our bed. We'll take the floor."

The couple swathed the stranger in their own thin blankets. They chafed his hands and feet.

What had come over her husband? Ellen wondered as she prepared gruel at the hearth. She'd never seen Jack like this—thinking of others. But astonished though she was, Ellen said nothing.

When at last the man's eyelids fluttered open, he gazed at Jack and Ellen from clear blue eyes. Then he slept. Ellen lay down on the floor, close to the hearth. Jack stretched out beside the bed.

Toward dawn, Jack woke with a start. At first he didn't know where he was. The dark cabin was light as the church on Christmas Eve, with a hundred candles burning.

Then Jack remembered the stranger. He jumped to his feet. The bed was empty, Ellen still asleep. But there in the light stood a young man in white robes. He had long feathery wings. His hair gleamed like gold.

"Don't be afraid," the young man said as Jack shrank back in terror. "You and I have met already."

"You and I—where?" asked Jack, pinching himself to see if he were awake.

"In Dead Man's Gully, last night," the man replied. "Have you forgotten? You carried me home. You gave me your bed, shared what you had."

"Who—who are you?" Jack faltered, staring at the stranger's blue eyes. They were exactly like the old man's!

"I am your Guardian Angel," the visitor said. "I knew of your surly ways, your uncivil tongue. So I tested you in the gully. When you answered my cry for help, I knew you were not *all* bad. There is still hope of Heaven for you."

Jack hung his head. He thought he was dreaming—but no, the

angel was speaking again. "For your kindness to a wretched old man, I give God's blessing to this house. And you, Jack, may make three wishes. Ponder them well. Heaven can be yours for the choosing."

As Jack weighed the angel's words, he found himself struggling between his promise in the gully, and those troublesome fellows who coveted things that were *his*. What he wanted was *protection*. That was only practical. Heaven seemed far off. Besides, Jack thought, there wasn't any reason why he shouldn't have protection, and keep his promise, too!

Jack looked up and saw the angel searching his face. Jack hesitated a moment, then said, "By the hearth yonder is my elbow chair. My first wish is that any man who sits in it shall be unable to rise—until *I* say so!"

"All right, Jack." the angel sighed. "Your first wish is granted. You have two left."

Jack studied his wooden wall box fondly. "That box holds my hammer, my thread and awl for mending brogues," he said without hesitation. "Every good-for-nothing who comes in wants to mend *his* shoes at my expense. My second wish is that anyone who reaches inside my box shall find himself stuck—until *I* let him go."

"Your second wish is granted," said the angel, sighing again. "There is still time. Choose your last wish wisely. You have one more."

This one will be fun, thought Jack, his face flushed with pleasure. He pointed to the sycamore outside the door.

"My third wish is that the next stranger to cut a cane from my tree shall find his fingers locked to it—until *I* set him free."

The shining youth gazed at Jack sadly. "Your three wishes exclude you from Heaven," he said. "But God's blessing on your house may save you from yourself."

When the angel vanished, Jack must have slept—though of this he wasn't sure. When he opened his eyes Ellen was bending over the hearth. Something tasty sizzled in the pan.

From that day the couple never lacked for food. The farm prospered. The calves and lambs increased. The chickens laid eggs, the cows gave milk. Jack's orchard overflowed with apples, his bins with grain. The young farmer never turned a beggar from the door empty-handed. To strangers he offered shelter and food.

Ellen never ceased to wonder at the change that had come over

Jack. She never learned of the promise her husband made that night in Dead Man's Gully. Jack never told her about his three wishes, for he had no occasion to exercise his wish power.

After many years passed, Ellen died. Jack lived alone in the cabin. His black hair was streaked with gray. He walked with a cane.

One night, as Jack sat in his elbow chair, puffing his pipe, he heard a sharp rap on the door. Before he had time to call "Come in," a dapper demon in a tight-fitting black suit strode into the cabin. Jack saw that he carried his tail over his arm, as jauntily as a walking stick.

"Good evening," said the demon, stepping up to Jack. Though the monster's manner was civil enough, his eyes had a threatening glint.

He's a *young* demon, thought Jack, observing his caller's slim figure, his short horns. Aloud, the old man said, "Welcome, stranger. What brings you here?"

"I've come a long way to fetch you to my master, the Devil," said the demon. "His kingdom is under the bottomless lake, far down in Mangerton Mountain. We'd best start at once. It's a long way from here."

"Aye, a long way, and a cold night," said Jack rising. "For any-one so important as your master, I must wear my best suit. I won't be a minute," he added as the demon tapped an impatient hoof. "Sit down, friend, in my elbow chair. Rest while I change," Jack said hospitably. "Warm yourself with a mug of my own home brew."

The demon sat down, sipping his drink with relish. With a show of haste, Jack pulled his clothes from the chest.

"Tell me," said Jack, buttoning his jacket. "Why did your master send for me?"

"Oh, that's easy to explain." The demon grinned. "He heard you were excluded from Heaven, and—"

"He wants me to visit him," Jack finished, reaching for his stick. "Well, I'm ready. Let's be off."

The demon tried to spring from his seat. But to his mortification he discovered that the seat of his trousers was glued to the chair. The harder he tried to rise, the more ridiculous he looked. All he could do was beat the air with his arms.

"Help me, help me, you wicked old man," screamed the demon in fury.

"Not until you've enjoyed my hospitality," cried Jack, tossing his jacket on the floor. He lifted his flail off the peg and then showered blows on the demon's back, as if threshing wheat. *Wham-m-m!* The flail fell on the creature's shoulders until he squirmed and twisted with pain. Smackity—smack—*smack*. Jack's blows fell like hail. The demon's shrieks echoed over the moor.

Only when the wretched monster begged for mercy, when he vowed he'd never return, did Jack's arm slacken. "Get back to your master," he roared, with a final wallop. "Get out of my chair, out of my sight. I've stared at your ugly face long enough."

The terrified demon—now scarcely able to drag his bones—crawled to the door, trailing his tail.

When the young demon, more dead than alive, slunk back to the Nether World—without Jack—the Devil's rage knew no end. *"What!"* he roared, stamping his cloven foot. "You can't be trusted to bring back *one* miserable mortal! You are too stupid to ever leave here again."

So speaking, the Devil booted the demon toward the fires. "All *you're* fit for is stoking," he roared, thrusting a shovel into the offender's shaking hands. Then Satan summoned his craftiest demon.

"You're to bring Jack here at once," the Devil yelled. His tail switched with anger. "Mind you, no excuses! Keep clear of that chair. And if you fail," bellowed Satan, his eyes shooting sparks, "I'll toss you into yonder fire—with my own hands."

The demon zoomed up to earth, without waiting for more. When he reached Jack's cottage, the old man was sitting by the fire. "Come in, come in," Jack called when the demon stamped up beside him. Aha, thought Jack, eying the demon's frayed gray tail. This one's old. I'd best take care.

"I'm taking you back to the Nether World with me," announced the monster with a leer. "And no tricks, this time. My master's in a hurry."

"I'll be ready in no time," Jack said. "But before we start such a long journey, I must mend my shoe."

The demon had no chance to object, for Jack kicked off his brogue. He pointed to the flapping sole. "One stitch will hold it," he said, "if you'll kindly hand me thread and needle, from that box on the wall."

89

The demon, thinking there was no harm in humoring his victim, reached into the mending box. But when he tried to remove his hand, it stuck. He couldn't move it one way or the other, no matter how he struggled and strained.

With a roar of pleasure, Jack jumped for the flail. He dealt cruel heavy blows on Satan's second messenger. The beating Jack had given the young demon was nothing compared to what the old one got. Whack—whack—whackity—*whack*. The flail thumped and thwacked, first the big ears, then the thick back.

At last the monster had to admit *his* craftiness couldn't equal Jack's. "Let me go," he screamed. "I'll never come back, if you'll show mercy."

"*Mercy!*" taunted Jack, enjoying himself immensely. "*That's* something you wouldn't understand! But take your fingers out of my box. Crawl back to your master. And if I ever see that face of yours around again," he added with a tremendous slap, "you'll get worse than this, my friend."

When the Devil learned how Jack had outwitted his craftiest demon, he fumed and raged so the monster blanched with fright. But in his heart, Satan was all the while thinking, Here's a mortal with whom I'd like to match wits. "I'll teach that oaf a lesson," the Devil muttered, taking a notch in his belt. "*I'll* bring him back in a wink."

The Devil had no sooner decided to fetch Jack himself than he whizzed up to earth through the Hole of Hell—as folk call the bottomless lake in Mangerton Mountain. It was a bright sunny morning when Satan arrived on earth. The air was frosty and cold, the ground sparkling with ice. With the swiftness of wind, the Devil sped to Jack's door.

"Well, this is an honor," cried Jack, hobbling to the door. "Imagine the Devil coming himself, for so humble a man!"

With a bellow Satan grabbed Jack by the neck, then pushed him down the path. "Get going, old fool," he ordered. "We've a long way to go."

"Aye," whined Jack. "A long way—and I must have my cane."

"That you shall not," snorted the devil, blowing out brimstone. "None of your tricks! Come along quickly, or you'll be sorry."

"But I'm an old man," whimpered Jack. "The road's slippery

with ice. If I fall and break a leg, *you'll* be the loser. You'll have to carry me on your back."

The more Jack protested, the harder Satan pushed him. But when Jack flatly refused to go another step without a cane, the Evil One listened. "At least, you can let me cut a branch from yonder tree to support my feeble legs," Jack cried, pointing to the sycamore.

"I'll fetch you a stick," yelled Satan, his horns quivering. "Maybe *that* will stop your tiresome complaints."

So speaking, the Devil strode to the tree. He grabbed a stout limb, and started to cut it. But when he tried to lower his arm, it was as if the tree held it in a vise. The more Satan tried to wrench himself free, the tighter his fingers clutched the branch.

With a yowl of delight, Jack ran back to the house for his flail. He thrashed the fiend until sundown, without pausing for breath. Jack battered and bruised him until pain racked the Devil's frame, from the tip of his forked tail to the tip of his horns. It was only when the huge glowing eyes were burnt-out embers, and the long red tongue hung like a rag from his mouth, that he begged for mercy.

"Let me alone," Satan gasped in a feeble voice. "I'll never bother you again."

"Well, then," cried Jack, with another smack, "what about taking me to the Nether World?"

"I don't want *you* there!" the fiend shouted, alarmed. "I'll bar you forever from Hell."

"That's better," said the old man, straightening his back. "And the quicker you get out of that tree and home, the better I'll like it."

After Satan had limped off groaning, Jack returned to his house and hung up his flail. Then he sank down to rest in his chair. Thrashing the Devil was the heaviest work he'd ever done, Jack told himself. He felt drowsy and tired.

While he dozed, Jack heard someone call his name. Opening his eyes, he saw the angel standing beside his chair. In one hand he held a lighted lantern.

"Take it, Jack," said the angel. "You're tired—but it's time to go."

"Go where?" Jack cried, his head muddled with sleep. "You told me I couldn't go to Heaven. The Devil doesn't want me in Hell. Where *else* can a body go?"

91

"Out into the world," said the angel sadly. "Until Judgment Day, you must wander the earth. Wherever you go—whenever people see your light in the night—they'll say, 'There goes Jack o' the Lantern.'"

Jack o' Lantern still travels this earth, as every Irish peasant knows. Everywhere boys and girls know it, too. That is why, on All Hallows' E'en, the night ghosts and witches flit through the sky, children carve Jack's features on scooped-out pumpkins, and put lighted candles inside. Then they race through dark streets, swinging their lanterns. It's in memory of Jack the Wanderer—not good enough for Heaven, too troublesome for Hell!

10

THE GIANT WHO OVERSLEPT
(Netherlands)

In the Dutch province of Gelderland is an ancient region folk call the *Veluwe*. It lies southeast of Lake Yssel, once the Zuiderzee. In the Veluwe the heather heaths, wide and rolling, glow with the purple of kings. There are forests of birch and pine, where bright birds make their home. At dusk, ghostly fawns leap among the trees. These are some of the wonders you'll see in the Veluwe. But you'll also see *hullen*, or hills.

In the level land of windmills and dikes, wherever you see a hill, you'll find a tale to explain it. *This* is the story of two hills in the Veluwe, the Great Hull and the Small One, and of the giant who made them. You can still see the hills—one of them big, the other little. They lie on either side of the road, halfway between the villages of Uddel and Elspeet.

Today firs and scrub oaks cover both hills. But long, long ago, when giants inhabited the heath, people say that the hills were heaps of sand. Then they tell about Ubbink, the Giant of Uddel, who lived near the forest, and Jolink of Elspeet, the Giant from Hardenberg Hill.

The two giants were friends. Together they caught fish in the lake, and shot wild boars in the forest. Both giants were huge fellows, though Ubbink was the bigger of the two. *He* stood so tall he could peer over the top of the tallest pine, so strong he carried saplings on his back as if they were faggots. His arms were so powerful he could pick up a hundred-pound stone as easily as a pebble.

In spite of his size and incredible strength, Ubbink was a gentle, slow-moving giant. He never stole sheep or oxen. He never plundered the land. He lived with his wife, Griet, in a hut he'd scooped from the earth, then thatched with heather boughs. After supper, when the day's work was done, the giant mended his nets or sharpened arrows for his bow. Then he slept soundly until gray morning light crept under the door.

Ubbink lived in peace with everyone. Only Thunar, the thunder god, was his foe. Thunar hated giants. He had vowed vengeance against all their race. "They're an evil lot," the god muttered, as he charged through the sky in his goat-drawn chariot.

Thunar's hatred of giants so twisted his mind that he saw no difference between good giants and bad. "The only good giants are dead ones," he roared, thinking of Ubbink. *His* peaceful plodding ways infuriated Thunar until he longed to destroy him.

"Look at the bumbling fool," the thunder god yelled to his goats. "He's too stupid to fight me, even when I tease him. I've a mind to crack his witless head!" Thunar recalled the time he had blown sand into Ubbink's eyes, until the clumsy fellow upset his day's catch of fish in the water. He'd been on the lake all day. The giant's eyes smarted so tears ran down his cheeks—but he didn't even protest!

Thunar snorted with disgust, then tossed his gleaming hammer into the black sky. Like jagged streaks of lightning, his weapon flashed through the clouds. When Thunar caught the hammer again, the earth shook until birds hid their heads under their wings, deer ran in terror.

As Thunar idly toyed with the hammer, he burst into boisterous laughter. "I've used you, my beauty, to split mountains open," he cried as he caressed the long jagged blade. "You have felled the mightiest oaks in the forest. Now you're going to do something else to amuse me. You shall smash Ubbink's bread oven into a thousand bits. *That* will hurt him worse than to crack his slow-witted pate!"

Thunar well knew Ubbink's pride in his bake oven. He knew the giant's weakness for bread. Why, he'd seen the hulking creature devour twoscore loaves in a day! Thunar had watched Ubbink build his oven, a few yards from the door of his hut. For days the fellow had fetched stones from the river bed. He had panted and sweated to pull them up the bank. Then he had set the stones in place, one on another. He had smoothed them with loving care. In the hearth underneath, Ubbink burned saplings. On the hot stone slabs his wife, Griet, baked his bread. The thunder god laughed cruelly. Yes, indeed. Ruining the oven would be just the thing.

That very night Thunar drew on his shining war helmet. He leaped into his chariot. He snatched up the reins. Zigzags of fire tore the clouds apart as the god brandished his hammer over his head. Shrieking with terror, the long-horned goats plunged through the night. The chariot wheels screamed and grated as the creatures careened toward earth.

Ubbink, asleep in his bed, heard the clatter. He tossed and turned. The boom-boom of a terrific crash brought him straight up in bed. "That Thunar is riding low over the heath tonight, with no thought for the sleep of others," he muttered. Then he covered his ear with a pillow. In another minute he dozed off again.

It wasn't until morning, when Ubbink rose to fetch wood from the forest, that he discovered what Thunar had done. When he opened the door to step outside, he saw the destruction. Fragments of rock and stone, torn branches of trees, lay scattered over the ground. Where his beloved oven had stood, a deep hole yawned in the heath. The giant stared at the rubble. His huge body trembled with anger. He clenched his fists so his nails bit into the flesh.

"So Thunar was here," Ubbink shouted, when he could speak. "What I heard were his hammerblows on my oven!"

The giant shook with helpless fury. Then, overcome by Thunar's vengeance, he wept tears of rage. "My oven, my beautiful oven," he moaned in despair.

Griet, wakened by Ubbink's laments, rushed to his side. She found him slumped on a stone, rocking his body slowly back and forth. "My oven," the giant repeated dully. "It will take weeks to repair it—and then, what is the good? Thunar is ruthless. He'll only wreck it again. And meanwhile, what shall we do for bread?" Griet's arms went about her husband as she tried to comfort him.

But in spite of everything Griet said, Ubbink refused to be consoled. The more she endeavored to soothe him, the louder the giant groaned. Only when she advised him to ask help from their friend Jolink did her husband look less hopeless.

"Jolink has an oven," Griet reasoned. "Tomorrow is his baking day. Why don't you ask him to bake *our* loaves, along with his own? He won't refuse help in our need."

Cheered by Griet's sensible words, Ubbink pulled himself together. Before long he was running across the heath to see the Giant of Elspeet.

Jolink and his wife, Bartje, greeted their friend warmly. "Of course, of course," the Giant of Elspeet boomed, when he'd heard

Ubbink's story. "What are friends for? Besides, my oven's big enough for *two* batches of bread. Bring your unbaked loaves here by six in the morning. You'll have bread in time for lunch."

"If you do the baking, I'll fetch the wood," cried Ubbink, eager to do his part. "Griet told me we could count on you."

"As surely as we can both count on Thunar's vengeance," Jolink muttered darkly, shaking his fist at the sky. "This won't be the end of his tricks—unless we outwit him!"

"Outwit him," repeated Ubbink. "*Who* outwits Thunar, or escapes his hammer?"

"*We shall*," thundered Jolink, winking at his friend. "Just wait until we build your new oven!"

As Ubbink started toward the forest he was still wondering what Jolink meant. With every sapling the giant twisted from the earth he muttered, "I wish *this* were Thunar's neck!" But exercise cooled his anger as the hours sped toward dusk. By the time Ubbink hoisted a huge bundle of trees to his back, he'd forgotten his wrath.

Jolink and Bartje met their friend when he returned. They helped ease his burden to the ground. Then they urged him to rest by their hearth.

"Stay to supper with us," Bartje urged. "Our porridge is bubbling in the pot. Sit down and eat before you go home."

Ubbink was so tired that he needed no persuasion. After the giants had eaten enough to satisfy four-and-twenty men, they scraped their wooden bowls until they squeaked. "And now," cried Jolink jovially, "we'll drink a toast to tomorrow, while Bartje scrubs the pot."

Joiink poured out the ale, then lifted his mug. "To the success of our baking," he rumbled, thumping Ubbink's back.

"And to outwitting that fellow in the sky," shouted the Giant of Uddel, draining his mug at a gulp. At the next toast his friend proposed, Ubbink clapped his great hands.

"To the oven Thunar's hammer can never break!"

One toast followed another in rapid succession, as the giants sat by the fire. It was almost midnight when Ubbink staggered to his feet. At the door his friend shouted, "Tomorrow at six! Don't forget."

"And mind you aren't late," warned Bartje. "We have to shut the door, once the oven's heated."

"I'll not be late," Ubbink mumbled as he headed for home.

The Giant of Uddel, who glowed with Jolink's ale, his friend-ship, the warmth of his fire, felt quite cheerful now. Things would all come right, he thought. Griet's advice was good. Jolink had proved he was their friend. And as for that sneaky Thunar—they'd get even with him!

It was late when Ubbink reached home. But in spite of the hour, his heart felt as light as the pale wisp of smoke that rose from the hearth. The giant sniffed the air, fragrant with the scent of rising dough. He lifted a corner of the napkin that covered the trough. Good girl, he thought affectionately. Griet had set the sponge. She'd left everything ready for an early start to Elspeet.

As the giant rolled into bed, he took care not to waken his wife. Almost at once he fell into deep sleep. His ear-splitting snores soon rasped through the night. The noise was so tremendous that the roof shook. The snores echoed across the countryside for seven leagues about. Ubbink slept soundly, without thought for the morning. It wasn't until he felt more light than usual through his closed lids that he jerked his eyes open with a start.

At first Ubbink stared about wildly, not remembering where he was, or what troubled him. Then he leaped from bed with a shriek of dismay. "Quick, Griet," he shouted, dragging her from the covers. "*I have overslept!* I must be at Elspeet by six. Already the sky is light."

Ubbink darted to the door. He peered across the heath. "I can see faint smoke rising from Elspeet," he groaned in despair.

Griet was working furiously at the trough. Her hands flew as she kneaded the dough, then formed it into fat round loaves. Ubbink loaded them to a board as fast as Griet made them. Then he made for the door, the board balanced on his head.

"I'm late—*late*," Ubbink wailed as he started for the road. "With this load, I'll never reach Elspeet in time."

"Oh, yes you will," Griet encouraged from the door. "There *is* time, if you hurry. Only you must take care not to upset the loaves in the sand."

For what seemed like seven weeks of Sundays, Ubbink ran across the heath. He didn't pause a second. He thought of nothing but reaching Elspeet in time. "I'm almost halfway," he gasped, scan-ning the sky anxiously. "If I keep up like this, I *can* be there by six."

The words were scarcely out of his mouth, when Ubbink felt

his feet drag. His shoes were made of lead, not wood! "What *can* be the matter?" the giant groaned. "My feet are so heavy, *I can't make them run!*"

The giant had to slow down to a stride, then to a crawl—for no reason, so far as he knew. It never occurred to him to examine his feet! Though Ubbink strained every muscle in his immense legs, it wasn't long before he couldn't lift them an inch. He stopped, unable to move. Though he struggled until the sweat poured down his brow, Ubbink stood rooted to the heath.

Only then did the slow-witted giant think to glance down at his feet. He shouted with relief at what he discovered. His wooden shoes—which were big as barges on the canal—were packed with sand to the top!

"Ah-ha," cried the giant. "If *that's* all that weighs my feet down, I'll soon be running again."

Ubbink balanced the board on his head with care, then leaned slowly to the right. Gradually he managed to work his foot free from the great wooden shoe. Then he tipped the clog over. The sand that rushed out made a heap that grew bigger and bigger. By the time the giant was rid of the last tiny grain, the heap was big as a hill.

Ubbink slipped his foot back inside the shoe, then leaned to the other side. The sand that flowed from the second clog made *another* hill—not quite so big as the first.

"Now I'm off again," grunted the Giant of Uddel, wriggling his toes. "And how I must hurry," he cried, with an apprehensive glance at the brightening sky. From across the heath, he thought he could hear Jolink scraping his trough. With feet as light as the morning mist now rising from the heath, Ubbink sped toward Elspeet. His long legs covered the distance so quickly that more sand flew out of his shoes than in! Thump—thump—thumpity—*thump!* The giant's feet pounded the heath with thuds so deafening that Jolink and Bartje heard them.

"He's coming," shouted Jolink. "I told you to wait. He's almost here!"

"We'll wait," Bartje cried, her hand on the door of the oven. "He's late, but we'll wait for his bread."

As Ubbink panted toward them, Jolink cheered. "Here he is." The Giant of Elspeet ran to lift the heavy board from his friend's

99

head. Together they shoved the loaves inside the oven. Bartje swung the door shut.

"We celebrated so well last night," Ubbink said with a sheepish grin, "that this morning I overslept."

"But we heard you coming," guffawed Jolink, slapping the giant's back.

"And you'll have bread as usual today, in spite of Thunar," said Bartje, smiling.

"And every day," rumbled Jolink, "until we finish your new oven."

The giants set to work on the oven soon after. They labored in secret, night after night, when the moon rose high in the heavens.

"We can't let Thunar know what we're up to," chuckled Jolink. "We'll work on the nights *he* stays in bed!" Craftily, the giants built the oven *under* the ground. Then Jolink roofed it with thick slabs of turf. From a distance, the top looked like a mound of earth—nothing more.

When the oven was done at last, Jolink and Ubbink danced around it until the heath quaked under their heavy feet. "This is something Thunar can't smash with his hammer," Ubbink cried, rubbing his great hands in glee.

And he couldn't, of course, though Thunar well-nigh split himself with fury, the night he discovered the new oven the giants had built under the heath.

After hundreds and hundreds of years, Ubbink and Jolink—and all other giants—vanished from the Veluwe.

But even though giants no longer live on the heath, the Great Hull and the Small One still remain. You can see them, just where the Giant of Uddel poured sand from his clogs, when he carried his loaves to Elspeet.

11

THE ENCHANTED WOLF

(Ireland)

Once upon a time, in Ireland's Kerry County, Neddy O'Leary, a poor peasant lad, tried to wrest a living from his tiny farm on the slope of Mangerton Mountain. Though he rose each day at dawn, and toiled until dark, Neddy never could get ahead. It seemed as though *pookas*, the bad fairies, were bent on his ruin. One misfortune followed the heels of another, until Neddy thought he was bewitched.

First, he broke the point of his plow on a stone. Then—after he had cut the wheat with his scythe, and winnowed the chaff in the sun—his five bags of grain disappeared in the night. But the worst came a fortnight later. When he went to the barn to milk his cow, she was lying dead in the stall. And, as if that weren't enough trouble for one day, he discovered his sheep strangled on the hillside behind the house.

"A demon haunts this farm," Neddy told his sweetheart, Maggy Flanigan, one day. She had brought him a firkin of butter she'd churned with her own hands, thinking she would wheedle Neddy into taking her to Corran Fair, and maybe buying her a necklace of glass beads.

"It's as plain as can be," Neddy said. "Demon or spirit—I'll find out tonight. I'll take my blackthorn stick to the field when the clock strikes twelve. There I'll wait for the creature—and do him in."

"Oh-o-o-oh!" wailed Maggy, as she rushed into Neddy's arms and buried her red curls in his shoulder. "Take care—oh, do take care. The c-creature might do *you* in," she sobbed, making a great show of her fears.

Though he secretly quailed at the thought of encountering an unknown demon alone, in the dead of night, Neddy felt himself a hero—with Maggy in his arms. For three years now, he'd begged her to be his wife. Maggy had promised, but there was always an excuse to postpone the wedding. "When you're better fixed on the farm," or "When you've saved enough for those earrings we looked at yesterday." Once Maggy had stroked Neddy's freckled nose and coaxed, "If you'll take me to town next week, "I'll let you pin a brooch on my bodice, and put a bow in my hair."

Maggy always wanted things that cost money—money Neddy never had. He thought he had lost the girl, but here she was, fretting over him! He held her closer, then dried her tears. He'd fix the Thing, he told her, with a boldness he didn't feel. Be it fairy, fiend or man, he'd strike first! When Maggy left for home, she turned and threw Neddy a kiss. He waved back gaily, then sat down by the hearth to think.

As dusk closed in, Neddy trembled with fright. Resolutely he filled the kettle, then set it on the hob. "I have only a few hours to wait," he told his cat. "I'll fix my tea. What a feast I'll have, with Maggy's butter on my bread!" The cat purred loudly, rubbing against Neddy's knee.

Maggy's fears warmed the youth's heart. He put his feet on the fender, then gulped down hot tea. After seven cups of the strong black stuff, and seven slices of bread thickly spread with butter, Neddy felt he could fight anything. Maggy would marry him, once his luck changed! How he'd ever replace his dead stock, the lad didn't know. Yet, once he caught the Thing . . .

As Neddy sat by the fire, the hands of the clock crawled toward midnight, the hour when pookas and spirits roam. Who—except a demon—could wish him ill? Neddy wondered. No one in the village, surely. Why, he and all his family were born there. They were friends with everyone.

Glancing at the clock for the hundredth time in the hour, Neddy sprang to his feet. He tightened his belt. He snatched up his worn jacket. Then he strode toward the door with his blackthorn stick.

The moon shone brightly on the field where Neddy no longer had any sheep. The night was still. Not a blade of grass stirred. Not even a bat or an owl flew through the air. Neddy paced the pasture slowly, peering this way and that. He kept a sharp eye on all stones, on the dark copse that fringed the field. Spirits always lurked in such places!

Neddy glanced behind a black boulder, then back to the moonlit patch at his side. What he saw startled him so that he thought he had taken leave of his senses. For there, next to him, stood a young man! Neddy could neither scream nor run. Finally, when his breath came back to him, he stammered, "Who—who are you?"

"It's a fine night," remarked the stranger, paying no attention to Neddy's question.

"With a f-f-fine moon," agreed the youth shakily. He clutched his stick firmly thinking, I'd best find out who the fellow is, before I knock him down. From what he could see, the stranger was no ordinary intruder. His manner was civil. He had noble bearing. And yet—there was a strange look to his eyes.

As Neddy gazed into them, *the man disappeared.* In his place stood a huge wolf. The monster had long gleaming fangs, and a lolling red tongue that seemed to be dripping blood. Neddy shrieked in terror. Then, mustering all the strength he had left, the youth made the sign of the cross. After that, courage flowed back to his heart.

"Don't be afraid," the wolf rumbled in a hoarse growling voice. "I won't hurt you. I am the man who stood at your side. I'm enchanted! If you do as I say, I'll make you rich—so rich Maggy will marry you."

Neddy was still shaking as he stared at the wolf. The monster's eyes glowed like lanterns in the night. Those fangs looked so ferocious— they'd bite a man in two.

"T-tell me wh-what you want me to do?" the youth quavered at last.

"The wicked witch inside Mangerton Mountain changed me into a wolf, when I discovered her lair," said the beast. "She put a seven-year spell on me. She forced me to kill your cow and strangle your sheep," continued the wolf, hanging his head. "She threatened a horrible death unless I ruined you and your farm. She's hated you, it seems, ever since you chopped down her ash. Help me, Neddy. I can help you."

All the while the wolf was speaking, Neddy was thinking, Maggy would marry me in a minute if I were rich. The anguish he saw in the creature's eyes—and his longing for Maggy—moved Neddy to say, "I'll help you all I can. Tell me what to do."

"Follow me then," said the wolf, turning toward the glen below the mountain. "You'll never regret your decision—if you do as I say,"

he added. He trotted across the field ahead of Neddy, and then plunged through the copse. After ascending a slope, the wolf stopped abruptly before a sheer slab of rock. He raised his great forepaw. Then he rapped three times, calling, "Open door, open to me."

With a suddenness that racked the whole mountainside, a door flew open. Dazzling light blinded Neddy. When he recovered, he found himself standing inside a gleaming chamber, lined with gold from ceiling to floor. In the middle of the room was a gold table, set for two, with gold plates and goblets and wonderful foods. The wolf had vanished. In his place, beside Neddy, a handsome young man stood. He had shining blue eyes, hair golden as the walls of the chamber, and he was dressed royally.

"Sit down," said the youth, leading his guest to the table. "We'll eat as we talk." Neddy, too dazed by the splendor to reply, sat down on a golden chair.

"I am a Prince," said his host, filling Neddy's goblet. Then he waved his hand about the room. "Gold shall be yours—as much as you want—if you'll promise never to tell its source. If you keep this promise for seven years, you shall have endless riches and honor, and I shall be freed from the witch's curse. But if you betray this secret," the Prince continued in a terrible voice, "poverty and ruin shall be your lot. While I—I shall be doomed to skulk through the night, a loathsome beast of prey, seven years more."

"I'll help you. You can count on my word," cried Neddy, clasping the Prince's hand. "Have no fear of betrayal by me. I'll not tell anyone your secret—not even Maggy," he promised. "*You'll* be a Prince to the end of your days. *I'll* win my girl."

After the youths had drunk a toast, the Prince rose. "This gold is yours," he said, giving Neddy a small bulging bag. "Take it. Use it as you see fit. When you have need of more gold, return to the glen. Knock three times on the rock. Speak as I did, and the door will open. Now farewell, but remember—if you break your promise, if you reveal the secret of your wealth, we are both lost."

The next thing Neddy knew, the morning sun was streaming through the window of his cottage. What a strange dream I had last night, the lad thought, as he jumped from bed. Then he caught sight of a small bulgy object on the floor. "It's the bag of gold!" he shouted, staring at it. His encounter with the enchanted wolf, his promise to the handsome Prince, and these gold coins were no dream. "I'm a rich man—*rich!*" Neddy cried, unable to believe his good fortune.

Neddy set to work at once. He rebuilt his old tumbledown farmhouse. He made stalls for cattle, and pens for sheep. Then he purchased fine beasts at Corran Fair. He bought a new plow, and two oxen to pull it through the earth. He planted potatoes and wheat. Everything Neddy did prospered. At harvest time, his crops were the finest for miles around.

"Where did the lad come by such wealth?" the men whispered, when they met to drink at the Mermaid tavern. "Up to now, Neddy's never had two coppers to jingle in his jeans."

Though gossips wagged their tongues from morning to night, Neddy took care not to break his promise. He went about whistling as he fed his fat pigs. He sang as he guided the plow. When he thatched the barn, his humming rivaled that of the bees in the clover.

Maggy had set their wedding date. Soon he'd bring his bride home. Neddy was so happy he paid no attention to the girl's curiosity about his sudden wealth. "I came by it honestly," was all he'd say when Maggy wheedled and hinted, or accused him of finding treasure in his field. "Honesty is all that matters," Neddy would say, rumpling her shining red curls. Then he would talk of their wedding plans.

The more Neddy evaded her questions, the more determined his sweetheart was to learn his secret. Had he found a pot o' gold at the rainbow's end? she wondered. Maggy remembered her grandmother speaking of such treasure. Perhaps Neddy had come upon a hoard belonging to the Wee Folk, or perhaps . . . The girl's curiosity consumed her. She had to find out!

Maggy took to spying on Neddy after dark. From the window of her house in the valley she could see the lights of the farm. Sometimes she hid in the bushes, watching the youth at his chores. But in spite of peeping around corners, and trailing Neddy here and there, she never discovered any clue to the riches.

Late one night, as Maggy sat by her window staring toward the farm, she saw a light bobbing across the field. "That's Neddy's lantern," she exclaimed. Hastily wrapping herself in a shawl, she ran out the door. Now the light was moving toward the copse that bordered the pasture. "If I keep well behind him," Maggy muttered, "I may find out what's going on."

106

By now she had entered the thicket, where the light disappeared. Maggy parted the bushes. She crept along stealthily, fearful lest a snapping twig give her away. Neddy was somewhere ahead in the glen. The girl stopped when she heard three loud raps, then Neddy's voice calling out, "Open door, open to me."

There was a sudden bang, then such bright light that Maggy sank to her knees in terror. She was too frightened to move until—after what seemed like hours—she heard Neddy's steps coming toward her. In one hand he held his lantern, in the other a bulging bag that jingled as he walked.

"What crime are you concealing from your sweetheart?" Maggy shrilled, jumping out so suddenly that Neddy nearly tripped on a stone. "Tell me whom you're robbing—where you're getting your money."

"*Robbing!*" shouted Neddy, flinging the girl back. "How dare you come here? Why did you follow me to the glen?"

"To ferret out your secret," screamed Maggy, beside herself with rage.

"That I'll never tell you," cried the youth angrily.

"Then I'll never marry you," threatened Maggy. "If you have secrets *before* we're married, what will you do *after* we're wed? If you don't tell me where the gold comes from, you'll be looking for another bride."

Faced by the thought of losing his sweetheart, seared by her taunts, Neddy broke his promise. He grabbed Maggy's shoulders. Gazing into her flashing eyes he confessed everything. He told her about the enchanted wolf, the witch's spell.

Neddy had barely finished his story when Mangerton Mountain —which towered above them, black and forbidding—seemed to shudder apart. Flames leaped from the summit. Forks of fire shot into the sky. It was then that Neddy saw the enchanted wolf. He was standing in the licking flames. In the eerie light the monster's eyes glowed fiercely. They burned into Neddy's guilty soul.

"*You're* done for now, Neddy O'Leary," wailed the wolf. "And the witch still holds *me* in her spell."

From the depths of the mountain broke a triumphant shriek, then wild laughter that prickled the spine. At last, the witch chanted her awful curse.

107

"You, Prince, twice seven years a wolf shall be,
For Neddy, your friend, has betrayed you.
He'll roam Erin with a peddler's pack.
To honor and riches he'll never come back."

The witch had scarcely finished when an angry torrent burst through the mountainside. Neddy snatched Maggy up in his arms. He carried her to safety just as the waters crashed into the glen.

Once they had escaped the raging waterfall—which you can see to this day—Maggy screamed she'd never marry Neddy. For now she knew the lad had lost his farm. The gold she coveted had vanished forever.

It was then that Neddy picked up a peddler's pack. He trudged across Ireland from coast to coast. He sold pins and needles, buttons and thread. On lucky days, Neddy made enough for a meal. He slept under hedgerows beside the road. Now and then, he lodged at a mean inn.

So the years crept by, until Neddy was gray. Whenever he heard a wolf howl in the night, the old man wept bitter tears. For he always remembered the promise he had broken, the Golden Prince he'd betrayed—as well as his own self.

12

PETER AND THE FIRE-BREATHING DRAGON
(England)

Long, long ago, in Yorkshire's lovely North Riding, a dragon with an exceedingly hot breath lived on a hill overlooking the River Rye. At night the monster ravaged the once-peaceful valley, where the river flowed like a silver thread. Cottagers trembled when they heard his hideous bellows and hissings. They blanched with terror when his horrid howls echoed over the dale.

"The dragon is wandering the moors tonight," farmers muttered to their wives. "Tomorrow we'll find our sheep stolen, our corn scorched with his breath."

Death and destruction followed the dragon's raids as night follows day. People wrung their hands and shook their fists in rage. They huddled together in frightened clusters. "When he's done with our calves and lambs," they whispered, "he'll start on us. No one is safe."

When tales of the monster's plunderings reached the King, he didn't lose a minute. He dispatched a brave knight with all speed to cut off the creature's head. But the knight—who'd already destroyed a giant, killed a demon, and rescued a maiden from a dreadful witch— was no match for the dragon. When the dragon saw the knight approaching, he rushed at him with a growl, then broiled him with his breath. When the sword fell from the knight's hand, the monster coiled his long tail about him. Then he squeezed the knight to death.

Other brave men came after this unfortunate knight, to do battle with the dragon. None escaped alive.

When the dragon had devoured all the sheep and cattle, he started to attack the people. The King sent heralds throughout the land. He offered the hand of his daughter Rosamond, and half of his kingdom, to any knight who could slay the fiend.

One youth after another rode forth to conquer the dragon, for the Princess was so fair that each man was willing to risk his life to win her. Yet no knight ever returned alive. The dragon, more insolent after each killing, now roamed hills and dales at will.

One day, when the people were so desperate they'd given up hope, a shabby young man with a yellow dog begged admission at the palace gate. Though the lad insisted that he must see the King at once, the guards only laughed at him. What possible business could a poor country fellow have with the King? When they tried to make the stranger go away, he drew himself up proudly. "I shall talk with no one but the King himself," he declared. "And I shall not leave until I do."

At last the guards led the young man to the King's audience chamber. The dog trotted at his master's heels.

"Who are you?" roared the monarch. "What do you want? And what do you mean by bringing that cur into my presence?"

"My name is Peter," said the youth. "This is Tike, my dog. He follows me wherever I go. We have come to ask your Majesty's permission to do battle with the dragon."

"What nonsense is this?" the King shouted, half rising from his throne. He stared at the youth's serious face, at the small dog sitting on his haunches beside his master. Then the King threw back his head and laughed. "You're just a stripling," he cried. "You and your dog wouldn't make a mouthful for the monster. Go home, boy. The bravest knights in the kingdom have attempted to slay the dragon. All have failed. Even as we speak, vultures are picking their bones on the lonely moor."

"But *I* shall not fail," said Peter, regarding the King with unflinching blue eyes. *"I have a plan!"*

"And what makes you so sure *you* cannot fail?" the King asked.

"Because, Sire, with your help, I can kill the dragon through cunning, rather than force of arms," the youth answered. "Besides," he added, blushing to the roots of his fair curly hair, *"I love your daughter.* I want to win her as my wife."

The King, who had listened with attention at first, now bristled with anger. "You? A peasant? A vagabond? How dare you—*a nobody*—presume to marry a Princess, even if you *should* kill the dragon?" he demanded, pounding the arm of the throne with his fist. "Where are your arms—your horse—your spurs? Or do you intend to fight with bare hands?"

"No, Sire," Peter said slowly. "I have no arms, no horse. For them I beg your aid. I intend to *earn* my spurs . . . and your daughter. I am a poor orphan—but neither a peasant, nor a vagabond," he added with quiet dignity.

The King had to admit that the youth had noble bearing. He didn't shrink before the King's anger. Hidden fire smoldered in those clear eyes.

"My father was a knight," Peter continued. "He died in your service, Sire, when I was a baby. He carried your colors proudly—to the end."

The monarch's heart softened as he studied the youth. "Go on, Peter," he said kindly. "Perhaps I was hasty. Tell me what you want to do."

"My plan cannot fail," declared the young man with confidence. "But to carry it out, I need your help."

"Go on," repeated the King. He listened without interruption as Peter unfolded a daring scheme. The ruler's eyes burned with excitement, with sudden hope. He leaned forward on his throne as Peter talked. Here was a lad with brains as well as courage. Perhaps he *could* kill the dragon, after all!

When the youth had finished speaking, the King cried, "I'll start preparations at once. If your plan works, I shall welcome you as my son. My daughter, and half my realm, shall be yours."

Speaking thus, the monarch sent for the finest smiths, spinners and weavers in the land, to assemble at the palace. Under Peter's direction, he set them to work. They were to fashion a suit of mail, and an undershirt, such as no warrior had ever worn.

For thirteen days and thirteen nights the craftsmen worked at furious speed. The palace garden rang with the clatter of metal, the pounding of hammers, the smiting of steel. Spinners spun threads no fire could burn. Weavers wove them into a magic cloth.

Folk across the moors saw the fires burning. They sniffed the black smoke from the forges. They heard the whirr of spinning wheels, the constant bang of the looms. "Master hands are making Peter's wonderful suit," they said. "God grant the lad success. In him lies our only hope."

At last the armor was ready. The threads were spun, the cloth woven. The King and the Princess and all the court gathered in the palace to watch the craftsmen dress Peter.

"Now the fire-breathing dragon can't scorch his body," said the weavers as they slipped the magic shirt over the youth's head. "His helmet will keep the heat from burning his face."

When the smiths had finished putting on the glittering mail, the little dog growled fiercely. Tike didn't know Peter. He bared his teeth. He snarled like a wolf. Not until his master's voice from inside the helmet said, "Come, Tike, come. You and I have work to do!" did the dog's growls turn to joyous yelps.

Even the King and his daughter found it hard to recognize Peter in the strange armor. For it bristled with row upon row of sharp knives, from the crest of the helmet to the tip of the shoes. The blades stood out all over like porcupine quills. Each thin bit of steel glinted in the sun until the brightness dazzled the eyes.

Peter mounted his white horse at the palace gate. He turned in the saddle to salute the King. He smiled at the lovely Princess, who stood beside her father, her pretty eyes brimming with tears. The young warrior spurred his horse, then headed east, where the dragon lived on the hill.

"Dear Heaven, bring him back alive," whispered Rosamond, clasping her hands. She watched Peter disappear around the bend of the road. Through her tears she saw the little dog as a yellow streak behind the horse's hooves.

"He's a brave lad," said the King gently, leading his daughter into the palace.

For two days Peter sped across green rolling meadows. He covered the moors where purple heather grew. On the morning of the third day, he entered the country the dragon had scorched. Here the land lay barren and brown. Peter's horse picked his way with caution along the riverbank. He mounted a hill. There the youth slipped from his saddle. He gazed across the dale where gray stone farmhouses huddled among the seared trees. Then he stared at the hill behind him where sycamores marched toward the top like soldiers, two by two. Up there somewhere in the dense woods on the summit, Peter knew that the dragon lurked in his lair.

Turning to Tike, Peter said, "We've no time to lose. We must surprise the dragon." The little dog wagged his tail, then sprang toward the hill. Peter spoke to his horse. "Stay here," he said, patting the shining flanks. "Stay until we return. But if we *don't*," he added slowly, "go back alone to the King."

As Peter followed Tike under the sycamores, he unsheathed his sword. "It's sharp enough to cut the dragon in two," he said as he tested the edge. When he saw the little dog waiting for him at the edge of the woods, new courage surged through the youth's heart.

As they entered a thicket of briars and prickly thorns, both man and dog crept along slowly. Upon reaching a clearing bordered by rocks, Tike frantically snuffled and sniffed in the leaves. Then, with a sudden furious snarl, he leaped toward the mouth of the black yawning cave.

Soon hair-raising howls issued from the opening. Peter tightened his grasp on the sword. Scalding steam belched from the cavern, enveloping his body in thick burning vapor. But in spite of the deadly heat, the lad suffered no harm. His specially made armor protected him.

When the vapor had cleared away, Peter saw the dragon crouching in front of him, glaring from red fiery eyes. The monster, who was coiled round and round like a rope, sprang at the youth, wrapping his scaly green tail about Peter's slender body.

Then the dragon squeezed. But the tighter he pressed against Peter's suit, the deeper the knives bit into the monster's flesh. With shrieks of pain the dragon loosed his hold, until he fell back on the ground. There his long green body twisted and writhed. Blood dripped from ugly gashes in his sides.

When the wounded creature rolled on the ground, Peter leaped at him to sever the head from the body. To his horror, the steel blade glanced from the neck without a scratch. Peter soon discovered that the ground where the monster rolled contained some awful magic. As soon as the dragon flung himself down, his yawning wounds closed. The flesh healed.

While Peter was wondering what to do next, the dragon—by now completely restored—jumped at him with a howl. This time the monster was more determined than before to choke the breath out of his foe. But as the dragon squeezed tighter and tighter, the blades dug into him cruelly. He screamed with the hurt. He bawled with the ache until the topmost leaves on the trees trembled and shook. Then he fell to the ground. But before he could restore his strength by rolling on the earth, Peter hacked away the tip of the dragon's tail.

Tike, who was watching the fray from behind a tree, now darted out. He snapped the flying fragment in his jaws before it touched the ground. Then he dashed down the hill. The dog didn't pause until

113

he'd reached the place where the horse awaited their master. Still holding the tip of the dragon's tail in his jaws, Tike scrabbled up the soil. When he'd made a hole, he dropped in the fragment. He covered it with earth, then tore back to Peter's side.

Hour after hour, Peter fought the dragon. Inch by inch, the youth chopped his body to bits. One by one, the little dog buried them in ground that had no magic.

At last only the dragon's dying head remained. *"We've won,* little friend," Peter shouted. "We've won—thanks to *you,* to my armor and my shirt!"

The dog seized the head in his teeth. But the horrible thing was too heavy for him to carry. With his master's help, he tugged and pulled the head down the hill. Peter tied the trophy behind the horse, where all might see it. Then Tike grinned from one ragged ear to the other. With a yelp of triumph he leaped to the saddle—taking care that Peter's armor didn't cut *him.* There Tike perched, red tongue lolling, yellow tail flying, as the horse raced for the King's palace, with the dragon's head bumpity-bumping behind.

As they sped across the hills and valleys the fire-breathing dragon had scorched, farmers left their work to see the sight. They shouted thanks to their deliverers. Children scattered flowers in their path.

The King and Rosamond and all the court gathered at the palace gates when they heard the horse's feet pounding the road. "Long live Peter. Long live Tike!" they shouted as the returning heroes rounded the bend, dragging the monster's head.

The King stepped forward with open arms. "My son," he cried, "you have earned your spurs. You and Tike have earned our gratitude and love."

Turning to his daughter, the King placed her small hand in Peter's. "Your courage has won the hand, and also the heart, of lovely Rosamond," he said. "Half of my kingdom is yours."

After the wedding, Peter and the Princess—and Tike—lived happily forever after. As the years passed, people built a church above the River Rye, where Tike had buried the dragon. From the churchyard, to this day, you can see the wooded hill beyond the sycamores where Peter battled with the fire-breathing dragon.

13

THE MANTICORE OF NORTH CERNEY
(England)

Many hundreds of years ago, when the Romans marched in Britain's West Country, a pagan monster called a Manticore roamed the wooded hills about the River Churn.

The Manticore's name was Marcus. He was wild and free as any creature that ever bounded across the heights above the hamlet of North Cerney. Though the monster was huge, he was gentle. Still, he had a troublesome habit of wanting to see all living things wild and free as he.

Now Marcus terrified village folk because of his appearance. For the Manticore was half-man, half-lion. From his tawny hair to his waist, he was a handsome youth, with two arms, two hands. But the rest of his body was that of a beast. Short tawny fur covered the lean flanks, the four great feet, the tufted tail with its sharp hidden spike. The thick shaggy ruff that is a lion's collar surrounded the monster's waist.

People of North Cerney seldom glimpsed the Manticore—and then none too clearly. What they did see made them shudder with fright.

"A lion's roving our hills," women wailed, pointing toward the strange creature that leaped from crag to crag with the grace of a giant cat.

"*If* it's a lion," men said, turning pale at sight of the monster, "he has the shoulders and head of a man!"

In spite of their terror, the monster never did them any harm, though his passion for freeing captured creatures from chains and cages nearly drove farmers out of their senses. The man-lion loved freedom. At night, when he crept through the village on great noiseless feet, he unlatched henhouse doors. He let colts out to frisk in the moonlight. He undid the pens where pigs snortled. He let down the bars of folds where lambs cuddled beside their mothers.

Marcus shouted with delight and played his flute as he watched the freed creatures romp in the pastures. Sometimes—when the moon was big and round and bright—Marcus danced behind the animals in the meadows. In his deep stirring voice he sang of stars in the heavens, of mountain torrents that rushed to the sea.

The next morning, when farmers found their fowls and beasts in strange places, they shook their fists at the hills. They cried, "The Manticore was here last night!"

Yet for all their rage, farmers never found a sheep missing, a hen harmed. Still, because Marcus was such a strange-looking creature —a monster—they feared him.

As the man-lion bounded across the hills at night, he held his flute to his lips. Folk stirred in their sleep when the wind caught the clear notes. In the morning, no one—except some of the children— remembered the music they'd heard in the night. But a peculiar gladness lingered in people's hearts.

Today most of the inhabitants of North Cerney don't know the whole story of the man-lion. They can't even tell where he came from, or whither he went. But they point to his likeness, crudely scratched in the stones on the south transept wall of the church.

"That is the Manticore," they say, "the fabulous creature that Pliny the Elder, the Roman naturalist, described more than nineteen hundred years ago."

Pliny must have feared the Manticore. It's plain he never *saw* him, for the monster he writes of was horrendous. As to the image on the church, some claim this thing, others that. But *we* think a parish priest who loved Marcus carved his likeness long ago, to remind people forever after of a pagan monster's generous act.

It's likely the tale began the night little Tim Cooper suddenly woke from a sound sleep. Moonlight streamed through the window. The rays were so bright that Tim could see distinctly the red roses on his cotton quilt.

The child sat up in bed. He rubbed his eyes. Up and down his spine crept that *tingly* feeling he always got when something wonderful was going to happen. He had the same feeling the day he found golden flag-flowers down by the brook, the time the broken-winged robin let him be his friend. Only *this* was different—as if some greater life beckoned from the moonlit hills.

When Tim heard the wild sweet music, he knew he'd heard it before, in his dreams. Only now the music was *real*. This was no dream.

The boy leaped from bed. He pattered to the window in his bare feet. When he peered toward the hill, he saw a wonderful creature —a man with tawny hair, riding the back of a big yellow cat. As the man played the flute in his hands, the music floated toward Tim. It was so magic that it lured the child toward it. He longed to join the man.

"I'm coming! I'm coming!" Tim called. "Wait for me—oh, please don't go away."

The next instant, Tim scrambled from the window. Grasping the trunk of a stout vine with both hands, he slithered to the ground, and landed with a soft thud in his mother's pansy bed.

Tim picked himself up quickly. Then he ran toward the music. But it didn't stay in one place. The notes moved swiftly toward the pond, then to the copse at the pasture's edge, finally to the riverbank.

"Wait for me—*wait*—I'm coming!" Tim cried. He scrambled this way and that for what seemed a lifetime. Stones cut his bare feet. Dog-rose briars tore his hands. The music was now far away.

Tired and confused, the small boy sank to the ground. He could run no farther. Though he could hear the river babbling, the music had stopped. Tim was too turned around to know where he was. "I w-wa-want to find the music," he sobbed. "*Please* don't go away."

When Tim woke next morning, he felt strong arms about him. Even before he opened his eyes, he knew *the wonderful thing had happened*! A voice somewhere over his head was chanting a joyous song. Tim thought he was dreaming, for the voice was deep and clear as the silver trumpet he'd once heard at church, on Easter morning.

With an effort Tim's eyelids fluttered open. He found himself staring into the smiling face of a young man. Tawny hair framed the noble features. The eyes that met the child's were deep blue and kind.

"So you're the lad I found sobbing last night—after you lost the music," said the stranger, brushing the child's pale curls from his eyes. "What's your name? Where do you live?"

"I'm Tim," said the boy. "I live beyond the village—in the little thatched cottage with the purple flowers. I heard your music, and saw you riding over the hills on a big yellow cat. So I slid down the

vine. I called and called and asked you to wait. But I guess you couldn't hear me. The music kept moving. I got lost, and then—then—"

Feeling something furry tickle his toes, Tim glanced down. His eyes popped with wonder at what he saw. Until then, he supposed he was talking to a young man. But now Tim found himself staring at yellowish brown *fur*! He saw four huge legs stretched on the ground, four great cushiony feet—and a tail with a tufty end.

Tim wasn't frightened. He was puzzled, just the same. "I—I saw you riding a c-c-cat!" he stammered. "But *you're* the cat, too!"

"So I am," laughed his new friend so merrily that Tim laughed with him. "Lions belong to the cat family. I'm Marcus, the man-lion. From the waist down, my body is a lion's. That's why I run and leap and pounce like a big cat. I'm holding you in my two man-arms. It's my lion ruff that's tickling you. My feet are fleet and sure. When you sit on my back, I'll carry you far away over the hills with the speed of wind."

"Oh, do, Marcus, *do!*" pleaded Tim, throwing his arms around the man-lion's neck. "Take me with you. Play your music for me. I won't leave you—*ever!*"

"Yes, but what will your father and mother say?" Marcus asked, hugging the child.

"I have no father," said Tim. "He died a long time ago. And I've no one to play with since we moved from the village. My mother has to sew all day. She has no time for a little boy now. She used to take me blackberrying—tell me stories—help me make boats from horse-chestnut shells. But now she's always tired. She works by the window all day—sometimes at night by candle light. If I ask her to sing to me, she's c-cross," Tim sobbed. "I'm lonely. May-maybe my mother doesn't love me any more! I-I want to stay with you."

"So you shall," whispered Marcus, holding the boy closer. "You, too, must be free, little lad. And now, stop crying," he added, drying Tim's tears. "I made you a present while you slept."

Marcus held out a small flute cut from a reed. "This is for you," he said, placing the pipe in Tim's eager fingers, "because you tried to find my music. I'll train you to play, so in time birds will listen, wild creatures creep from hiding. With this flute, you'll never be lonely again."

"I'll never be lonely with *you*," cried Tim, fingering the flute.

120

He was so happy now, he thought his heart was going to burst.

In the days and weeks that followed his meeting the Manticore, Tim had no time to miss his mother. To the child each new day was more wonderful than the last. Marcus taught him such remarkable things. Tim rode on his back to high secret cliffs where the eagle hatched her young. He saw where spotted trout laid their eggs, snakes had their holes, foxes their burrows. Marcus explained mysteries of seed and bud, of fruit and flower. But above all, he taught the boy what it meant to be free.

"All creatures should roam this earth without fear of capture," Marcus told Tim fiercely, as he released birds from snares that men set to catch them, hares and foxes from traps that maimed their limbs.

To the lad their most glorious adventures were at night, when Marcus played his flute. Then he bounded over the hills by moonlight. He leaped across rivers. He scaled dizzy heights. And always his music flowed with a rapture that filled the child with joy.

During these wonderful rides, Tim liked best to stand up on Marcus' back. For the boy soon discovered he could curl his toes in the ruff and clasp both arms around his friend's neck. Standing thus, Tim could peer up at the stars as they sped through the night. He could feel the wind whip his hair, watch dark fearsome shadows rush past. He felt so *safe*, clinging to Marcus and gazing far ahead—first on one side, then the other.

Back in the village, where no one guessed what had happened to Widow Cooper's son after he wandered away, people searched for Tim in hills and woods, day after day, for many weeks. But when they found no trace—neither footprints nor clothing—they shook their heads. "Tim's dead," they told the widow. "He's fallen into the River Churn and drowned—or else some prowling beast has carried him off."

Yet despite what everyone told her, Tim's mother didn't believe her son was dead. "I'd *know* if he were," she said. "He's wandered away, but he's alive. He'll come back, if I pray hard enough."

The young widow worked harder than ever at her sewing. But no matter how tired she was, the villagers always saw the mother at dusk, climbing the avenue of gray beeches to the small church on the hill. Wrapped in her shawl, she knelt on the hard stone floor, to beg for her child's safe return.

"Dear God," the woman implored, her cheeks wet with tears, "bring Tim back to me. I love him. I need him. He needs me. I'll light a candle in the window every night, so he can find his way home in the dark."

When Widow Cooper left the church, she often paused to talk with Father Paul, the priest who lived in a cottage nearby. The mother insisted, "I know Tim's alive. He will return one day."

"Have faith, daughter. Continue to pray."

The priest—like the child's mother—didn't think Tim was dead. In the village Father Paul heard uneasy rumors. People were more frightened than ever when they caught sight of the Manticore. "Now the monster has *two* heads!" women cried, wringing their hands. The old man confided his suspicions to none, save the fan-tailed white pigeons which fluttered to his hand for corn.

"Marcus hasn't been here for weeks," the Father said thoughtfully as he stroked a bird. "Not since the night Tim disappeared—and now that folk claim he has two heads. I wonder. . . ." He had his own notions about the two heads.

Father Paul sighed deeply. He had loved Marcus—his "pagan son"—ever since that day in the hills when the man-lion found him, and saved his life. The priest was searching for rare simples to heal a sick child, when his foot caught in a root. He fell down unconscious—for how long, Father Paul never knew. But when he came to his senses, and saw what he *thought* was a lion crouched beside him, he lapsed into darkness again.

When the priest opened his eyes a second time, he was staring into deep blue eyes. He felt a cool hand on his brow, heard a trumpet-clear voice say, "Have no fear, Father. When you're able, I'll carry you home."

Father Paul remembered thinking he'd never seen such a beautiful face—the face of a pagan god! He sighed again at thought of his lonely friend—the last of his race in these hills. How often the priest had tried to draw Marcus closer to the world of men. "Now people fear you," Father Paul had said. "Once they know you, they will love you—even as I do. With the bonds of human affection about you, you'll not be lonely."

"No, Father," Marcus insisted. "I am too strange to live among men. I can bear no bonds. I must be free. I'll always have need to run, to stretch these great muscles, to play my flute under the stars. I must leap through the hills and feel the wind in my face."

Yet for all his refusal to mingle with men, Marcus loved Father Paul. And the old man missed his laughter, the music of his voice. He missed the midnight tap at his door, when Marcus brought the first strawberries from the forest, the first wild grapes, or golden marsh marigolds from the brooks, or honey in the comb.

"Gifts from the garden of the gods," Marcus said, his blue eyes sparkling with mischief.

"From the garden of the *One* God," Father Paul corrected him, as they settled down to talk. Toward dawn, Marcus always bounded toward the wooded heights, playing his flute.

It was so long since Father Paul had seen his friend—or even heard his music—that he thought, Marcus is trying to avoid me. If he *has* Tim, he knows I'll make him return the child to his mother.

One night, as Father Paul prayed for Tim's safe return, the priest heard joyous music. Rising from his knees, he peered toward the hills. There, in a patch of bright moonlight, he glimpsed the fleeting figure of Marcus. And pressed close to his back, his arms about the man-lion's neck, stood a little boy. His head bobbed excitedly from side to side as the great creature leaped across the heights.

The priest laughed in spite of himself. "There goes the two-headed monster the villagers told me about—and exactly as I suspected," he cried.

The rest of the night, Father Paul paced the floor in doubt. What if Marcus *never* brought Tim back? In the human child Marcus had found a playmate, a friend, to share his free untrammeled life. And as for Tim—what lad could resist the man-lion's charm?

Toward morning, the priest decided not to tell the child's mother—or anyone—what he now knew for a fact. "In his own time, Marcus will come to me," he said. "Meanwhile, the boy is in good hands."

But as weeks passed and Father Paul saw nothing more, he was troubled. Had Marcus decided to move north, where none would recognize the child? Or had some evil befallen the man-lion? Was Tim helpless, alone?

One night, as thoughts such as these tortured Father Paul, the door opened softly. There Marcus stood, Tim in his arms.

123

"Father, he's sick!" Marcus cried, laying the boy on the pallet in the corner of the room. "Will you care for him? He burns with fever. I'll fetch herbs, roots—anything you need—from forest or field."

"Fetch water from the spring," ordered the priest, bending over Tim.

After Father Paul bathed the child's hot head, rubbed his aching body, Tim dozed fitfully. Then the priest spoke to Marcus. "My son," he said sternly, "you must return this boy to his mother."

"That I shall never do!" Marcus cried fiercely, his eyes blazing with anger. "The child belongs to me now. He wants to be free. He loves *me*. He never speaks of his mother. He doesn't *want* to go home."

"He may think he doesn't—now. But Tim hasn't forgotten his mother. He needs her and she needs him," said Father Paul. "She should have him, though I can nurse him through this illness."

"Then do!" stormed Marcus. "Because if you don't—if you tell the mother where he is—I'll take the boy where no one can find him. He's mine, I tell you. He came to me of his own accord. No one—not even you—shall take Tim from me!"

"I give my word not to reveal your secret, my son," said Father Paul, for he saw Marcus wouldn't listen to reason. As he turned to the child, the old man saw misery in his friend's deep blue eyes.

"The boy will recover," he added quickly. "Never fear. It's some childish malady. I shall give him tender care. And you can soothe him with your music. If you play from those bushes outside the window, you can see everything—yet no one can see you."

As Marcus sprang for the door he said gratefully, "Forgive my anger, Father. I know I can trust you. You are my friend."

All night Father Paul bathed Tim's hot face. When he called for his mother, the priest whispered, "Soon you'll be in her arms—if I know the heart of your generous friend."

Next day, the child was no better. Beads of sweat stood on his brow. Even the music of Marcus' flute did not ease him.

As the child moaned for his mother, Marcus watched at the window, his heart heavy with grief. The boy is out of his head. He's never wanted his mother before, the man-lion thought jealously. Tim loves only *me*!

As day faded to dusk and long shadows fell among the beeches, Marcus was too wretched to hear footsteps approaching the church.

He barely had time to crouch down in the bushes before a young woman in black opened the door.

When Marcus glimpsed the woman's face, he felt uneasy. Those large brown eyes, the hair that caressed the temples under the shawl, the soft mouth—all were familiar! In sudden panic, Marcus rose from the bushes and peered through the window. He studied the face on the pillow. The likeness was amazing. No doubt of it—the woman was Tim's mother!

"So Father Paul has betrayed me!" Marcus muttered savagely. "He has told Tim's mother. He sent for her to come here. Well, she won't get the boy—if I have to take him away tonight."

But Marcus' anger vanished as he watched Father Paul. His face was anxious, drawn. It was plain to see the child was worse. Marcus was afraid. Tim was too sick to move. Besides, the priest couldn't have sent the woman a message. He had not left the lad all day—and she had not rushed to the cottage where Tim lay.

Marcus felt he must have a look at that woman again—to be sure. Stealthily he covered the few steps to the church. By stretching a little, the man-lion could peer inside the shadowy place.

There was the young woman, kneeling on the stones. She was talking to someone, though Marcus saw no one there. He scanned the dusky corners, the dim aisle. The woman was alone. Yet she was speaking. There were tears on her cheeks. Marcus pressed closer to the window. He wanted to hear what she said.

"Dear God, bring my boy back," the woman sobbed. "Keep him from harm. I *know* he's not dead, that he wandered away—perhaps in search of a playmate. Please make Tim want to come back. Let him know how much I love him."

Marcus crept from the window, unable to bear more. He must have time to think. What about the boy? Father Paul said he needed his mother. But *I* need Tim, Marcus thought bitterly. His mother lost her chance when the child came to me. She doesn't even know how lonely the lad was. Tim loves me, *me*—

Thus Marcus argued with himself, even as he stared at the tear-stained face and the supplicating hands of the woman—even after he watched her leave the church, her shoulders bent and her head low.

It was midnight when Marcus returned to the priest's cottage.

Though weary and spent, he was playing his flute. The man-lion sprang toward Father Paul, who beckoned from the door.

"The boy passed the crisis an hour ago," said the old man. "He is asleep and well."

"An hour ago?" Marcus asked. He touched the boy's curls tenderly. "I'm taking him with me," he said, gathering Tim in his arms. "We must hurry. The moon is waning. Dawn will soon be here."

"Where are you going?" Father Paul asked, though the clear blue eyes told him what he wanted to know.

"To Tim's mother," Marcus replied in his deep vibrant voice. "He needs her. That I decided an hour ago. No human child is free to wander as I do."

"My son," cried Father Paul, his face shining with belief. "It was at the moment you decided to take Tim home that he passed the crisis. It is a sign! God has rewarded your generous act by redeeming your soul."

"Then give me His blessing," said Marcus, kneeling before the priest. "That I shall need."

At the door Father Paul embraced Marcus. "What about you?" he asked.

"My heart shall always be here," said Marcus, his eyes on the child's chubby face. "I'll not return. Beyond these hills, I may find others of my race. But whether I do or not, I have my flute—and Tim has his. He and I shall be close, even when leagues apart. And now, Father, farewell, and thank you," the man-lion cried, springing toward the valley.

Marcus moved through the village on great noiseless pads. He didn't stop until he reached the outskirts. He paused at a small cottage where a candle burned in the window. "It's for you, little Tim," he whispered to the sleeping child, "to light your way home."

Marcus peered inside. On the cot in the corner Tim's mother lay, exhausted. Pale curls framed her tear-stained face. "You belong with her," the man-lion softly said as he lifted the latch and opened the door. He moved across the floor and placed Tim on the bed beside his mother. Marcus blew out the candle, then sped toward the hills.

As dawn tinged the sky with rose, Father Paul heard distant music. "Marcus, my noble son," he murmured, "your restless spirit shall find peace. People shall always remember your generous deed."

When folk in the village learned the man-lion's story—in the days that followed Tim's return to his mother—Father Paul carved the Manticore's likeness on the outside wall of the church. "For he's pagan no more," the priest said. "He belongs forever to this House of God."

Tim never forgot Marcus, or the wonderful things he had taught him about the beautiful world, and the right of wild things to be free. Even though the boy missed his friend sorely, he had the flute—and the music never failed to cheer him. He found it good to be with his mother again. And now the widow somehow always found time to sing to Tim, to tell him stories, to laugh with him—though she still had to sew most of the day to support the two of them.

Although many centuries have passed since the man-lion roamed the wooded hills of Britain's West Country, you can still see his image cut into the stones of North Cerney's church. The small stone sanctuary stands on the hill, beyond the avenue of old gray beeches. That is where I found the story of the Manticore to tell to you.

About the Author

DOROTHY GLADYS SPICER, well-known for her stories of folklore, has traveled extensively in Europe and the Orient gathering material from many countries. Distinguished writers and scholars as well as country people have contributed to *13 Monsters*. John Masefield told Miss Spicer about the image of the Manticore scratched on the wall of North Cerney's church and between cups of tea, Dame Sybil Hathaway, feudal chief of the Isle of Sark, related the harrowing tale of The Wicked Squire. A Dutch scholar showed Miss Spicer the region of the Giant of Elspeet and friends from the Dutch province of *mooi Drenthe* took her to the turf hut of Ellert and Brammert.

Miss Spicer lives in White Plains, New York. She is the author of many articles and books on folk festivals, customs and foods. She has also written *46 Days of Christmas* and *13 Witches*.

About the Artist

SOFIA, who has illustrated many fine books for children, adds excitement and shivery fun to *13 Monsters*.